pine needles?"

Alex asked Hillary in a rough, tender voice. "Because in another minute you're going to be flat on your back."

"Or maybe you will," she replied with a challenging smile.

"Better yet," he said, pulling her closer.

"Alex, we have to stop this."

He shook his head, pulling the rubber band out of her hair, so the waves could tumble around her shoulders. "I can't stop. You're addicting."

"Alex, that's enough. I can't keep up with you."

"The problem with you is that you don't have any romance in your soul," Alex whispered as he pulled her closer.

No, the problem was she had too much, Hillary thought.

Dear Reader,

Whether it's a vacation fling in some far-off land, or falling for the guy next door, there's something irresistible about summer romance. This month, we have an irresistible lineup for you, ranging from sunny to sizzling.

We continue our FABULOUS FATHERS series with *Accidental Dad* by Anne Peters. Gerald Marsden is not interested in being tied down! But once he finds himself the temporary father of a lonely boy, *and* the temporary husband of his lovely landlady, Gerald wonders if he might not actually enjoy a permanent role as "family man."

Marie Ferrarella, one of your favorite authors, brings us a heroine who's determined to settle down—but not with a man who's always rushing off to another archaeological site! However, when Max's latest find shows up *In Her Own Backyard,* Rikki makes some delightful discoveries of her own....

The popular Phyllis Halldorson returns to Silhouette Romance for a special story about reunited lovers who must learn to trust again, in *More Than You Know.* Kasey Michaels brings her bright and humorous style to a story of love at long distance in the enchanting *Marriage in a Suitcase.*

Rounding out July are two stories that simmer with passion and deception—*The Man Behind the Magic* by Kristina Logan and *Almost Innocent* by Kate Bradley.

In the months to come, look for more titles by your favorite authors—including Diana Palmer, Elizabeth August, Suzanne Carey, Carla Cassidy and many, many more!

Happy reading!

Anne Canadeo
Senior Editor

THE MAN BEHIND
THE MAGIC
Kristina Logan

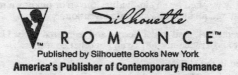

Silhouette
R O M A N C E™
Published by Silhouette Books New York
America's Publisher of Contemporary Romance

To my writing friends in Berkeley: Nancy, Lynn,
Sonia and Lucy, who provide great inspiration, lots
of support and delicious dinners.

SILHOUETTE BOOKS
300 East 42nd St., New York, N.Y. 10017

THE MAN BEHIND THE MAGIC

Copyright © 1993 by Barbara Beharry Freethy

ISBN: 0-373-08950-3

First Silhouette Books printing July 1993

Printed in the U.S.A.

Books by Kristina Logan

Silhouette Romance

Promise of Marriage #738
Hometown Hero #817
Two To Tango #852
The Right Man for Loving #870
To the Rescue #918
The Man Behind the Magic #950

KRISTINA LOGAN

is a native Californian and a former public-relations professional who spent several exciting years working with a variety of companies whose business interests ranged from wedding consulting to professional tennis, high technology and the film industry. Now the mother of two small children, she divides her time between her family and her first love, writing.

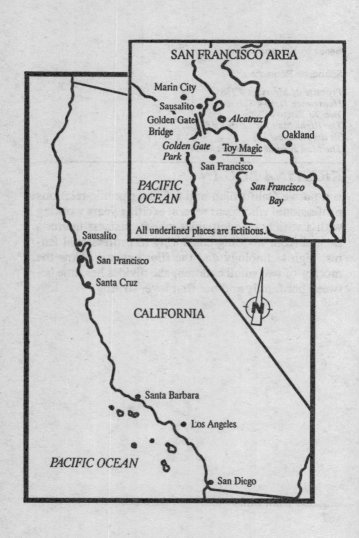

Chapter One

" " Ace Reporter Starts War on Santa Theresa.' " Roger Thornton, editor-in-chief of *World Today* magazine read the headline aloud and then tossed the newspaper down on his desk. He glared at the woman sitting across from him. "You're supposed to *report* the news, not make it."

Hillary Blaine crossed her legs and smiled nervously. "You can't believe everything you read."

"Very funny."

Roger took off his glasses and rubbed a hand across his weary eyes. He was a big bear of a man, well over six feet tall and at least two hundred plus pounds. In the past, Hillary had always considered his bark to be worse than his bite, now she wasn't so sure.

"I didn't do anything wrong," Hillary said, not quite able to look her boss directly in the eye. She knew as well as he did that her impulsive behavior on the island had instigated what otherwise might have been a very long standoff.

"You didn't do anything wrong? You started a small civil war, single-handedly." Roger smashed his fist down on the top of his desk, sending a batch of papers flying to the floor.

Hillary started at the motion, her uneasiness deepening. She had thought she would be able to explain, but it didn't look as if he was going to give her a chance. "I just wanted to get a little closer to the fence so I could see better. I didn't intend to start anything."

"You never do. But it keeps happening. Last time, you had half the city council members of that town in Minnesota up for recall. Now you cause a diplomatic incident." Roger shook his head back and forth as he stared at her. "The question is, what am I going to do with you? Tar and feather you out of town as some of my staff would suggest or..."

"Assign me to Washington, D.C.?" Hillary finished hopefully.

"Not on your life. You are so close to getting booted out on your..."

"Please, Roger, you have to give me another chance. I'm a good reporter. You know I am."

"I know you might be someday—if you live that long."

Hillary stared at him uncertainly. "Are you firing me?"

"I've seriously considered it. But I have to admit, reluctantly, that on occasion you do have flashes of brilliance, and I would hate to lose that. On the other hand, I can't afford to have you starting wars all over the world." He paused for a long moment, his eyes fixed on hers in an intimidating manner. "I don't want there to be any misunderstandings between us. I'm going to give you one last chance to prove yourself." He picked up a manila folder and pushed it across the desk to her. "Alexander Donovan."

Hillary picked up the folder, but didn't open it. Her instincts told her that the contents would not be good, not with Roger in this mood. "Who?"

"You know who. I want an in-depth profile on him for the January issue. Alexander Donovan is going to be our Man of the Year."

"Man of the Year?" she echoed in disbelief, her temper flaring despite the warning look in Roger's eyes. "For goodness' sakes, why? He's a toymaker, a playboy. This is not my style." Hillary tossed the folder back down on the desk and got to her feet.

Restlessness propelled her to the window. Ten floors below lay the busy streets of San Francisco, the place she had come to find her dreams. *World Today* magazine was one of the top news magazines in the country, focusing on serious issues, politics, foreign policy and the global economy. The cover story was usually a plum job, one she would ordinarily love to have, but Roger's choice of Man of the Year made the assignment seem ludicrous. She turned back to face him. "Just tell me why."

"Because you're a good journalist, Hillary, although sometimes you're too damned impatient."

Hillary stared at him for a long moment. "So now you're going to punish me with Alex Donovan?"

Roger smiled at the depression in her voice. "A cover story is hardly punishment. Besides, Alexander Donovan is rich, good-looking, an eligible bachelor, and he's local. You don't have to travel, and I can keep you on budget."

"He makes toys, doesn't he?" Hillary didn't even try to keep the disdain out of her voice. "I can't imagine why you want to make him Man of the Year. We should have a serious political figure on the cover, not a toymaker. I don't get it. Is the magazine changing focus?"

"He does more than make toys. He's a philanthropist. He donates thousands of dollars to needy organizations. In a time when people are cynical and depressed, he seems to be the embodiment of generosity and hope."

"In other words, he's a master of public relations."

"Don't close your eyes to the possibilities."

She threw up her hands in exasperation. "Are you telling me there's a bigger story?"

"I'm telling you to find out. I'll be honest with you. The magazine is hurting just like everyone else in this economy. Alexander Donovan is going to sell a lot more copies of our magazine than some overphotographed politician. The cover will bring in readers that don't normally pick up the magazine. Your job is to keep them reading. I want you to find out everything you can about this man, and not just what he wants us to know." Roger paused for a long moment, his eyes growing reflective. "I've met Alex Donovan a few times, and the man is very smooth."

Hillary studied him thoughtfully and perched on the edge of the chair in front of his desk. "You make him sound like a mystery. I'm sure he's been interviewed dozens of times."

"Three times this year. I have the clippings in the file, and each article says the same thing. Born in Los Angeles. Parents died in an automobile accident when he was a child. Raised by an aunt who also died. After that he made it on his own, no other relatives, not too many friends, just a lot of women who change with each party. I sense a facade here, something aside from his carefully cultivated background."

Hillary sent him a doubtful look, at the same time feeling her irrepressible curiosity kick into gear. "I would think all those deaths would be documented somewhere."

He nodded approvingly. "It's a place to start. I will say this. The man made his first million at age twenty-five, without the benefit of a college degree, and he hasn't looked back since. That was almost ten years ago. Last month he was ranked one of the twelve richest men in the country. He's a success story, and people like to read about success stories." He gave her a wicked grin. "Of course, if you discover a bona fide scandal or deep dark secret, better yet."

Hillary threw up her hands in defeat. "Okay, you win. I'll do Alex Donovan. I'll find out whether he's a saint or a sinner, and then we talk Moscow, right? Or I'll settle for the White House—anything with action."

"Right now you're just fighting to keep your job. Don't forget that. And no more gunshots or jail time, please."

"Killjoy."

"That's my job. Now do yours."

Hillary stood up and walked to the door of the office. "When do I meet with our Man of the Year?"

Roger checked his watch. "In one hour. I want to put this story to bed by October fifteenth. That gives you one month."

She raised her eyebrows. "It's Friday night. This incredible man doesn't have a date?"

"Only with you. And one last word of warning. Donovan is not a stupid man, and he has a great deal of clout. Use discretion, tact, and make sure you have all your facts before you put one word down on paper. The last thing I need is a lawsuit."

"I wouldn't dream of working any other way. And when I'm done, we'll talk White House." Hillary shut the door before Roger could answer and walked slowly back to her cubicle.

It was in the far end of the main newsroom and boasted one small window that overlooked downtown San Francisco. If she stood on her tiptoes at a certain angle, she could actually see the tip of the Golden Gate Bridge. Someday she would have a corner office like the senior staff members, with large bay windows and her own fax machine. Someday. If she worked hard . . . and she got the right assignments.

Sitting down behind her desk, Hillary tossed the file on top of the other paperwork she had to catch up on and idly spun the globe that sat on a corner of her desk. There would be no trips to the Caribbean this time, no earth-shattering story that would propel her to the top of her profession. She would have to be patient, and she had never been very good at waiting.

With a sigh, she reached for the file and flipped it open. A newspaper clipping slipped out, a color photo of a man and woman leaving a party. The man was dressed in a sleek black tuxedo. He was tall with dark hair, a square face, and a strong jaw. He was caught in midstride, the power of his movement clear even through the fuzziness of the photo. The expression on his face was a mixture of amusement and annoyance, and there was something about the thrust of his chin that seemed downright challenging.

Hillary turned the photo several different ways. Did his face really hide a mystery as Roger had implied? Or was Alexander Donovan just a good-looking man with too much money and too many women? Whatever he was, she could handle it. She could handle anyone, as long as he wasn't a complete bore. Dull and uninteresting would mean death to her career. Shaking her head, she closed the folder and twirled the globe with a wistful sigh.

* * *

"Here comes the big bad monster, and he's going to rip you into little pieces," Alexander Donovan said the words with greedy intensity as he pulled on the joystick of the video game, skillfully maneuvering the purple creature toward his opponent.

"No sweat." Rocky Aames pushed his control stick forward and, with his foot on the red button, sent the warrior jumping into space, neatly maneuvering around the marauding monster. "Way to go, dude."

"Not bad, but I've got you now." Alex made the monster do a sidestep and a fake, and then with one swoop, his monster gobbled the warrior up in his mouth. "You lose."

"That wasn't fair." Rocky pulled on the stick in utter futility. "How did you do that?"

"That's my secret."

"You're supposed to let me win. I'm only a kid."

Alex grinned down at his opponent's grouchy face, knowing his good humor and competitive spirit would reemerge within seconds. Rocky was just hitting puberty, gangly legs and teeth that were still a little big for his face. Pretty soon his voice would be changing and he'd be filling out, growing into his size-eleven shoes. The thought made him a little sad.

"You may be only twelve physically," Alex said, "but mentally I think you're about forty-two, which makes you seven years older than me. Besides, if you can't win this game too easily, I know I've done my job. This one should be a bestseller." He patted Rocky on the shoulder. "What did you think of my fake?"

"Not bad. You want to play another game?"

"Sorry, but I have work to do. What about you? Don't you have homework?" Alex stood and pushed the stool up against the video game. Then he walked over to his desk and leafed through the pile of mail that his secretary had brought in earlier that day.

"I'm done," Rocky muttered as he got up to put the video controls away.

Alex looked up and smiled at Rocky's downturned expression. The kid might be street smart but he was a terrible liar. "That's what you always say. How are things at home?"

"You mean at the Jenkins house?"

Alex caught his eye and held it, determined to read between the lines. Kids like Rocky didn't tell you anything outright. You had to see it in their eyes, their expressions, or the way they locked their arms around their waists. "They seem like nice foster parents. Are they treating you right?"

Rocky shrugged his shoulders and dug his hands into the pockets of his jeans. "They make me go to church on Sunday."

"Good. You could use some religion."

"And they want to see my report cards. I usually just throw them in the trash."

"All good things must come to an end," Alex said with quiet amusement. "You need school. It's important."

"But you didn't even graduate from high school."

"Yes I did, about six years later than I should have, but I got my diploma, and believe me things would have been a lot easier if I had just stuck it out the first time around."

"I guess. Do you want me to come by tomorrow and help you with research?"

"On Saturday? Don't you have something better to do?"

"The Jenkinses are going to visit some old lady. They don't need me around."

Alex sat down and sent him a thoughtful look, worried by the undercurrents in Rocky's tone. "Did they tell you that?"

"No, but it's not like I'm their real kid." He kicked at a spot on the carpet. "It's okay. I don't really care. They're better than some of the people I've lived with."

Alex nodded in agreement, wishing he could tell Rocky that everything would be fine. But would it? He knew firsthand how tough life could be, especially for a child alone. "Why don't you come by after school on Monday? I'm going to test the new crocodile squirt gun."

Rocky's face lit up. "Awesome. Can we do the train once before I go?"

Alex pushed the control box over to his young friend. "Sure, go ahead."

While Rocky started the train in motion, Alex checked his watch. Then, with a flick of his wrist, he turned the pages on his desk calendar to see what he had scheduled for the weekend. Dinner this evening, sailing on the bay on Saturday, another party that night, and brunch on Sunday morning. It should be enough to keep a reporter from *World Today* magazine happy. He could show her the wonderful, exciting life he led. She would be dazzled, and he would be Man of the Year. His smile turned into a frown. This would have to be his last interview for a while. He was beginning to believe his own press and that was dangerous.

Out of the corner of his eye, he watched the sophisticated model train begin its path around the office, through the tunnel under the chair, and over the file cabinet. He had come a long way. He could just forget about the early years. But even as the thought came to his mind, he knew it would be impossible to forget. His friendship with Rocky always reminded him of what he had left behind.

Rocky looked over at him in delight, his smile turning mischievous as they heard his secretary's voice outside the door. Alex gave a negative shake of his head, at the same time Rocky pushed the control box over to him.

"Do it," Rocky urged.

Alex hesitated, his fingers hovering over the button as he heard Rosemary's knock on the door. As soon as the door creaked open, he pushed the button. A shrill whistle lit the air, causing his secretary to take an abrupt step backward, one hand fluttering to her chest in alarm.

"Would you stop that," Rosemary Hill said irately. "You scared another five years off my life." She patted down her gray hair as she glared at him.

Alex laughed. "Does that mean you're now five years older or five years younger?"

Rosemary didn't reply, just pursed her lips in a manner that reminded Alex of an old memory of his mother. Maybe that's why he kept Rosemary despite her grouchiness and her bossy ways. She filled a void in his life.

"I suppose that was your idea?" Rosemary said to Rocky.

The boy gulped nervously, exchanging a look with Alex. "Not me, no ma'am."

"Maybe you should go on home now," Alex encouraged. "And do your homework, every last bit, so I don't have the Jenkinses on my case about letting you hang around here."

"I will," Rocky promised, bolting out the door while Rosemary simply stood there shaking her head.

"That boy needs more rules in his life."

"No. He needs more love." Alex looked down at the stack of papers she had placed on his desk. "What's this? I thought you were going to start handling the correspondence on your own."

"Those are all from women. I swear I don't know when you have time to work."

Alex pushed the letters aside. "You know I'm here every day from eight until six, sometimes earlier and sometimes later."

"Which means you must be doing an awful lot of socializing after hours." She held up a hand as he started to explain. "I don't want to know, so don't tell me."

"It's not that sordid."

"I hope not. That reporter should be here any minute now."

"That's right, *World Today* magazine, Miss Hillary Blaine." Alex leaned back in his chair as he thought about the interview he had agreed to. "I don't think we'll have any problems. I'll handle her just like I have everyone else. The publicity will be perfect for the launch of my new board game."

"Having this woman around for a couple of weeks is going to be a lot different than granting a one-hour interview. I don't understand why you agreed to it."

"They caught me in a weak moment, and they waved ten pages of free press in front of my eyes. I couldn't resist."

"She's going to be digging into your life."

"So, I'll throw her a few bones. Just enough to keep her happy. She's not going to find out anything about me that I don't want her to find out. I'm an expert at this, trust me."

Rosemary studied him thoughtfully. "Is there something to find out? Sometimes I get the strangest feeling."

"Don't be silly. I don't have anything to hide, or at least nothing that would matter to anyone but me."

"As the Man of the Year, I wouldn't be so sure about that." Rosemary crossed her arms in front of her plump frame. "I don't have a good feeling about this. My husband says Hillary Blaine usually covers politics and wars. She must be a tough lady.''

Alex shrugged as he pushed himself up out of his chair. ''I can handle her. If she starts digging in too deep, I'll just turn her in the other direction.''

''That would be easy if she were a dog on a leash, but I don't think she is,'' Rosemary replied.

''You never know.'' He grinned at her. ''Neither of us has actually seen this woman. If she's as hard as nails, she probably has a face like my aunt's old bulldog, a big pudgy nose and a fat pink tongue. In fact...''

He paused as the half-open door to his office was flung open abruptly. A woman stepped into the room. She was slender and blond, with snapping blue eyes that sparked pure outrage. Alex took an involuntary step backward. She hadn't laid a finger on him, but he felt as if he'd just been punched in the stomach.

''Who are you?'' he asked.

Hillary smiled grimly as she extended her hand. ''I'm the bulldog.''

Chapter Two

"Hillary Blaine." Alex said her name thoughtfully, while his gaze traveled slowly over her face. Now that he had a chance to catch his breath he had to admit that she didn't look a thing like a bulldog. Her face was pretty in a natural sort of way, with strong features and clear, engaging eyes that were sparking with anger. Although she couldn't have been more than five feet and a couple of inches, her shoulders were stiff and her slim body was poised in a way that exuded challenge. He exchanged a quiet look with Rosemary and then shook Hillary's extended hand. "I'm Alex Donovan."

"Of course you are," Hillary replied. "I already know your name. It's everything else that I'm here to find out." She put her briefcase down on his desk, sweeping his correspondence off to the side with a brisk motion of her hand.

Alex smiled. "Please make yourself at home."

"Thank you."

"This is my secretary, Rosemary Hill."

Hillary nodded in the older woman's direction. "It's nice to meet you. I hope we'll have time to talk, if not today then tomorrow. I'm sure you must have a different perspective on our Man of the Year."

"He's a good employer. That's all I have to say." Rosemary turned to Alex. "Do you need anything else tonight?"

"Maybe a bodyguard," he said.

Hillary felt a reluctant smile tug at the corner of her mouth. Her anger was slowly turning into a grudging admiration. Alex hadn't balked at her entrance, or even gotten irritated by her abrupt manner. In fact, he didn't seem off balance at all, while she felt as if she'd gotten on a roller coaster the minute she'd walked through the door. She had prepared herself for good-looking, but not sexy and charming, not this incredibly appealing hunk of masculinity. She cleared her throat, silently telling herself not to get carried away. After all, she'd been on a remote island for a few days. Any man was bound to look good.

She shifted her feet, waiting while Alex handed over several files to his secretary with last-minute instructions. His voice was quiet but firm and definitely edged with respect, deferring to Rosemary on a few minor points of organization. When they finished, Alex looked at her apologetically.

"Sorry for the delay."

"No problem. Shall I set up an appointment with you, Ms. Hill, before you go?"

Rosemary frowned, her brown eyes guarded and hostile. She was not going to be an easy mark. In a strange way, Hillary was pleased. It wouldn't make her job any easier, but it was nice to see that the playboy at least respected efficiency, brains and loyalty when it came to choosing a secretary. She would give one point to Alex Donovan, but it was going to be a long game. Bulldog, indeed.

"I'll be around," Rosemary replied. "Good night."

Hillary waited for the door to shut behind Rosemary and then turned to Alex, covering her uneasiness with assertiveness, the best way she knew to get results. "Are you ready, Mr. Donovan, or shall I wait outside?"

"I'm ready—for anything."

His confident tone was filled with underlying challenge, and it was impossible for her not to respond. "Good. I think we should set some ground rules before we begin."

Alex raised his eyebrows quizzically. "Really? What sort of rules?"

"As to how we'll proceed. Since we're going to be spending some time together, I think we should decide just how we're going to fill it. For instance—"

"I have decided." Alex cut her off in midsentence. "You're free to follow along on my activities, but they will be activities that I choose, not you. I'm only consenting to do this interview because I happen to enjoy reading your magazine." He smiled at her disbelief. "I do occasionally stop playing with my toys long enough to study world events. However, to get back to your point. Any rules governing our interview will come from me. You may ask any question that you like, and I in turn will answer any question that I like."

Okay, so he was going to be tough, Hillary silently acknowledged. She would just have to work harder and be patient. Lord, she hated that word, but she knew it was necessary. The man was too smooth to reveal anything to a reporter. She would have to bide her time, wait until he let down his guard. With any luck it wouldn't take too long.

"Well?" Alex prodded, waiting for her to reply.

"Whatever you say. Obviously you're the boss."

"And you don't like it one damn bit, do you?"

Hillary didn't answer, caught up in the expressions playing across his face. She had expected slick and sophisticated, prepped by the publicity photographs she had seen of him. She hadn't expected deliciously rumpled hair and sexy green eyes or a loose-fitting tie and rolled-up shirt sleeves that revealed tanned, muscular arms. What would it feel like to get caught up in his embrace? She let out a belated breath, suddenly realizing the turn her thoughts had taken.

Never! The word screamed at her. Hadn't she learned anything in the last six years? Hadn't one good-looking playboy been enough? She shook her head and deliberately broke the connection between them. "My personal feelings about this assignment are irrelevant."

"How can you say that when you're going to be writing a subjective piece?"

"It's not going to be subjective. It's going to be objective, the facts of your life and your business."

"As you see them," Alex finished. "I'm curious about your attitude. You don't seem very happy to be here. If I offended you with that bulldog remark, I'm sorry. I had no idea you were standing there."

"You're not sorry that you said it, only sorry that I heard you." She sent him a direct look and waited for him to squirm, but he didn't, and it was rather disconcerting. Instead of anger she saw a small smile playing across his lips.

"Would it surprise you to know that I was very fond of my aunt's bulldog?"

His smile grew broader and more persuasive, and Hillary had to fight with herself not to respond. She decided to change the subject. "What plans do you have for this evening, Mr. Donovan? My boss mentioned something about dinner."

"Yes. I have reservations for six o'clock at the Crystal Terrace."

Hillary nodded with appreciation. It was just what she had expected. "Very nice. But you don't have to try to impress me. I'm much more interested in the real man than the image."

"Really? Then you're the first in a long time. Let me sign one letter, and then we'll go."

Hillary nodded as he read quickly through the correspondence on his desk. While she waited, she glanced around the room, suddenly realizing how different it was from the standard office of a president. There was a large video game in one corner that would look more at home in a pizza palace than an office. A pair of strange-looking robots sat on one of the file cabinets and a model train track wound around the office.

"You can start it if you like," Alex said quietly.

She looked at him in surprise and then followed his gaze to the toy train. "Oh. No, thanks, I couldn't."

"Why not?"

"I've never played with trains. I grew up with a sister and mother who both thought the only toys appropriate for girls were dolls and play kitchens."

"Then you've missed out."

"My mother would not agree with you on that point."

"But I bet you would." Alex eyed her thoughtfully as she offered a noncommittal shrug. Then he reached over to flip on the switch. They were both silent for a moment, watching the journey of the train.

"My favorite story growing up was 'The Little Engine That Could,'" Alex said. "I see my life a little like that train, just chugging away toward the top of the mountain."

"I would think your career is more applicable to the flight of a jet airplane than a slow-moving train. You made your first million at twenty-five, and ten years later you're the Man of the Year. If that's not moving fast, I don't know what is."

Alex grinned. "You might have a point, but speed is a relative thing. Some people enjoy a slower pace. I never have. What about you? Are you on a fast jet or a slow train?"

"Me? I think I'm on a horse going backward."

Alex burst out laughing, a genuine smile crossing his lips. "You're very honest, aren't you?"

"Yes." She put her hands on his desk and leaned forward. "I hope you'll be just as honest with me. I want to do an in-depth story on you, Mr. Donovan. I'm not interested in trite little phrases you've said hundreds of times over the last ten years. I want more from you."

He didn't even flinch. "Why? What's in it for you?"

"A good story, what else?"

"I think there's something more."

Hillary tipped her head in acknowledgment. "Maybe I just want to get that horse I'm on turned in the right direction. Can we go now? I'm starved."

Alex nodded. "After you."

The Crystal Terrace was just what Hillary had expected, plush burgundy red carpeting, glittering chandeliers, a lot of business suits and solicitous waiters. Her filet mignon was cooked to the right shade of pink, and her every whim had been catered to. Obviously a big tip was in order. It was a good thing Alex Donovan had deep pockets. But then his celebrity had been well noted throughout the meal.

Various men and women had made their way by the table, stopping to offer a warm greeting or chat about some upcoming event. It had irritated her in the beginning, but as the meal progressed, she began to feel as though she was watching a well-rehearsed play. It was almost as if Alex Donovan had told these people beforehand that he would be dining with her and to come by and say something positive.

Of course, that idea was absurd. Why would he go to all that trouble to impress her?

She took another sip of her wine as Alex quietly ate his meal. He had answered a few bland questions easily, but they hadn't gotten into anything deeper than his birthdate and favorite author. She was going to have to do better, much better. But how? Maybe a startling question, something to get an honest reaction out of him, she decided.

"Tell me, Alex," she said, offering him a winning smile. "You don't mind if I call you Alex?"

"Of course not, Hillary," he said, mimicking her polite tone and insincere smile.

"I'm sorry," she said abruptly. "I don't think we have any need for false attitudes here. We both want the same thing—a good story. Why don't we get down to it?"

"I thought we were."

"Yes, well . . ." She paused, trying to think of a way to get a reaction out of him. "How did you feel when your parents were killed in that auto accident? You were about twelve, right?"

"I was devastated, as all children would be."

His tone was completely neutral, his eyes carefully guarded. Hillary waited for an additional comment, but none was forthcoming. "What happened to you after that?"

"I went to live with my aunt, my mother's sister. She was very good to me. Unfortunately she died when I was seventeen. I've been on my own since then."

Hillary nodded. Of course. That's exactly what his bio had said. But where was the emotion in his answer? Why couldn't she get a feeling for what he had felt, a young boy left all alone? It didn't add up. "Maybe you'd rather not talk about this right now," she said. "Perhaps we should leave the more intimate subjects to when we're alone."

He cast a look over his shoulder and then dropped his voice suggestively. "Now that sounds interesting. Just how intimate are we going to get?"

Hillary flushed, an irritating habit that she had never been able to get rid of. "That's not what I meant."

"Too bad. Actually, I don't have anything more to add. The past is in the past, and I prefer not to relive it."

"I see." It was another smooth, predictable answer. She felt like screaming. Instead she looked down at her empty plate and stabbed her fork at the last grain of rice. With that gone, she leaned over to spear an errant carrot on the side of Alex's plate.

His hand came down on her wrist in a harsh, unyielding grip. "Don't do that. Don't ever do that."

She looked at him in amazement, the intensity in his voice catching her completely off guard. Finally she dropped her gaze down to the carrot. "I'm sorry. Were you going to eat that?"

"Yes."

A look came into his eyes that made her catch her breath. Finally, there was emotion, pain in his eyes, a remembrance of something old, something that must have hurt him deeply. She didn't know what to say. His reaction was so out of character and in such ridiculous proportion to her meaningless act. She cleared her throat, trying to ease the tension in his face. "Can I have my hand back now if I promise not to trespass again?"

Alex looked down at her wrist trapped in the grip of his hand. He slowly eased the pressure and then pulled his hand away, shoving it into his lap with repressed anger and some embarrassment. "I'm sorry. If you're still hungry, we can order something more. They make an excellent chocolate mousse here. Or carrot cake, that's always been my favorite."

Hillary waited for him to stop talking, and her silence forced him to look into her eyes. "Are you all right?"

"I'm fine." His answer was so curt, she decided prudently to let the issue drop for the moment.

"Okay."

"Do you want something else to eat?"

"No."

"Then I'll get the check." He motioned for the waiter and handed him his credit card. "Tomorrow, I've made plans for you to see how I spend my weekends, meet some of my friends."

"All right."

"There's a party tomorrow night. We can go over that when I pick you up in the morning."

Hillary frowned at the way he was taking control of the situation. "Why don't I meet you at your place? I'd like to see where you live."

"Fine," Alex said evenly, having totally regained command of his emotions. He gave her the address. "Do you know the area?"

"I think I can find it. Shall I just look for the biggest mansion on the block?"

"It's large, but not quite the biggest."

"You mean there are still a few goals left for Alexander Donovan to accomplish?"

"A few." He sent her a curious look. "What about you, Hillary? What kind of goals do you have for yourself?"

"Me?" Hillary laughed nervously. "I'm a reporter doing a job, and I'm not the one being interviewed."

"Have you always been a reporter?"

She sighed as he continued the questioning. "Yes, since I was ten and started the first fifth-grade newspaper at Hazelton Elementary School."

"Fifth grade. That gives you quite an impressive history. What got you started?"

"My father was a foreign correspondent. I grew up hearing about the power of the press. When my fifth-grade teacher decided to penalize the girls who wore pants to school, I decided a newspaper story would be sure to change her way of thinking. Unfortunately all I got to write was 'I'll mind my own business' five hundred thousand times. Once again, my timing was off. A year later, they changed the dress code."

Alex smiled at the rueful expression in her blue eyes. For a moment he saw a hint of another woman, not the outwardly tough female reporter, but a softer, more vulnerable creature. He had never met anyone like Hillary before. Her style was one of mannish efficiency. Her blond hair was pulled back in a stark ponytail, and her black dress belted at the waist was the essence of simplicity. The only hint of something different was the speck of lace peeking out of the bodice, and that bothered him. It seemed a contradiction in terms, just as the vulnerability in her eyes seemed to go against her tough, ambitious exterior. Who was she, really? And why did he care?

The answer hovered on the tip of his tongue, but he refused to admit the thought into his mind. He had spent a long time learning not to care, especially about people who could hurt back. And this woman certainly had that capability. She could write anything about him, stir up all kinds of trouble if he didn't watch his step.

"You didn't learn your lesson very well, since you're still sticking your nose into other people's business," he said.

"But it is my business," Hillary replied. "Back then I was too young and too intimidated to fight my fifth-grade teacher, but now I'll keep after a story, especially if it will make a difference."

"And who decides that? You?"

His skeptical tone put her nerves on edge. "The public has a right to know."

"Not good enough. We both know that some stories will have you walking a very fine line."

"I can keep my balance."

"I hope so. I don't happen to believe that everyone has a right to know my deepest secrets."

"Then why give an interview?"

"Because I don't mind sharing my insights on my business and to a certain extent, my life, my philosophy, and my future goals. But I don't really understand why anyone would care whether I squeeze my toothpaste from the top or the bottom."

"And which do you do?"

Alex shook his head and started to chuckle. "I don't think my bulldog comment was too far off the mark. You're going to make this difficult for me, aren't you?"

"Not if you tell me what I want to know." She leaned forward, her blue eyes sparkling from their exchange. Alex caught his breath at the sight, feeling an unmistakable pull between them.

He wanted to look away, but he couldn't find the will to do so. He had a sudden urge to touch the smooth skin of her cheek, to find out if she was warm or cool, to see if she would blush for him again, if her eyes would turn dark with emotion. It was a crazy thought, and his fingers twisted a knot in his napkin as he thought about giving in to the impulse. She would be shocked and angry. But it might be worth it.

"Hillary." He paused, watching the sparkle in her eyes turn to uncertainty. He dropped his voice down to a husky whisper. "I want—"

"Your check, sir." The crisp words of the waiter caught them both off guard and Alex sent the man a blank look. "What?"

"Your check." The waiter pushed the booklet toward Alex and stood patiently by the table.

"Oh, of course," Alex replied, not sure whether he felt relieved or angered by the interruption. As he busied himself with the task of adding the tip and compiling the total, his common sense reasserted itself, and by the time he had finished, his guard was carefully back in place. He couldn't afford to be attracted to Hillary Blaine. She was only with him because she wanted a good story, and he was only with her because he wanted the press and publicity for his new board game. Putting anything else into the picture would complicate things. He handed the booklet back to the waiter and turned to Hillary. "Shall we go?"

She nodded pleasantly, hiding whatever she was thinking behind her cool smile.

Hillary was silent on their drive back to his office. She should have been asking questions, finding out what Alex liked to do in his spare time, what type of music he preferred, maybe asking him why he didn't want to share his food and why he had looked at her in such a way that made her heart stop beating.

She swallowed hard at the memory of his words "I want." She couldn't imagine what the rest of his sentence would have been ... *I want to see you again...I want you to get the speck of lettuce out from between your teeth...I want to take you home and make love to you.*

Lord, no!

She must have had too much wine. Okay, so it had only been one glass. She had a light stomach and a light head for even thinking of Alex Donovan in those terms. He was her interview subject. As Roger had reminded her not so long ago, she was supposed to report the news, not make it. She needed to find the woman who was Alex Donovan's lover, not become that woman.

She pushed the automatic button, lowering the window to let the cool night air blow across her face. It had just been so long since a man had looked at her with desire in his eyes. Or maybe she hadn't noticed. She had dates like everyone else, but few men understood her dedication to her work, her desire to do something worthwhile with her life, and Lord knows she had never been able to share her fears about intimacy, not after her foolish fiasco with Douglas Wilmington. Even now, six years later, it was a painful memory.

She took a deep breath and let it out, trying to regain her objectivity and her control. She had to stay sharp and unemotional. It was absolutely critical.

"Are you all right?" Alex asked, sending a curious look in her direction. "It's cold out there."

"It feels good," she said, focusing on the lights of downtown rather than on his intriguing face. She had to get over the crazy feeling that had somehow developed in the pit of her stomach. She had to concentrate on getting this job done and moving on. Her career depended on it. "What time shall I meet you tomorrow?" she asked, trying to regain her perspective. "I'll bring my tape recorder along, if you don't mind, and then I won't have to take notes."

"I do mind, Hillary. No tape recorders."

His tone was very definite, but Hillary was not easily intimidated. "May I ask why?"

He stared straight ahead for a long moment, considering the question. "I prefer a more personal approach."

Hillary sucked in a deep breath. She was not going to touch that statement, not tonight, not with the way she was feeling. "I presume you don't mind a pencil and notebook."

"Only if you can keep it unobtrusive. This is a social event. I don't want my friends to feel uncomfortable."

"What exactly are we going to do?" Hillary asked with a growing sense of unease. She was never going to get good answers in the middle of a party.

"Something I enjoy very much." He turned to look at her and grinned. "Don't look so worried. It's not X-rated."

"I'm not worried." She infused a note of casualness into her answer. "I'm sure I can handle anything you have planned."

"That's probably true. Didn't you just get out of the middle of a war or something?"

Hillary felt the familiar red wave climb her neck and spread across her cheeks. She looked out the window at the passing lights and wondered why only the mistakes she made seemed to be well-known. "Who told you that?"

"I did my homework."

"Then you know what happened."

"Only the bare bones. Something about an overly ambitious reporter getting impatient with peace talks."

"There were no peace talks. There was nothing going on. It was a standoff."

"Until..." he prodded.

"Someone had to make a move."

"And you did it."

"Not deliberately. It wasn't like I fired a gun or something," she said, refusing to look into his face. She didn't want to see the skepticism there or, worse yet, amusement. "Sometimes you have to take a few chances to get the real story. That's all I was doing."

"Why don't you tell me your version?" Alex suggested. "I'm interested in how you work."

Hillary turned then and sent him a squelching glare. "As I said before, I'm not the one being interviewed, and as for my work, you're welcome to pick up any back copy of *World Today* and read one of my articles."

Her words created a long pause between them, and Hillary wondered if she had been too abrupt, too harsh. After all, she was supposed to be making friends with the man, not creating an antagonistic situation. "I'm sorry. I didn't mean that the way it sounded."

"I was just trying to be friendly."

"It's better if we keep things strictly business."

"You're right. Strictly business is the way to go."

It was the answer she wanted, but when it came it was very unsatisfying. What had she expected? That Alex Donovan would declare a burning desire to get to know her better? That was never going to happen. She had watched and listened as her older sister went on date after date. She knew what men liked in a woman and it certainly wasn't brains and a flat chest. Maybe she'd filled out a bit since adolescence, but where her mind had gotten sharper, her dates had gotten fewer. Maybe that was the problem. Her hormones were kicking up and Alex was a good-looking male. That didn't mean she had to do anything about it.

If only he wasn't turning out to be nicer than expected. She wanted to dislike him. It would be easier to dig into his life, to rip him apart if she had to.

"We're here," Alex said, cutting into her thoughts. He pulled into the parking lot under his office building. "Which one is your car?"

"The red Mazda."

"Interesting." Alex pulled his car into the empty space next to hers.

Hillary unbuckled her seat belt, ignoring his look of speculation. "It gets me where I want to go."

"You could get where you want to go in a brown sedan, Hillary. I think a person's car says something about their style. After all, a car is in many ways an adult toy."

"Then why do you drive a black Mercedes? It seems rather dull for the Toy King."

Alex smiled with understanding. "It's respectable. My investors like it. I have a four-wheel-drive Jeep that I use for pleasure. I take it up in the mountains, and then there's no place I can't go. It gives me complete and absolute freedom. Maybe I'll take you for a ride sometime."

"Sure, why not? We're supposed to get to know each other."

"Yes. I must admit you're not what I expected."

Hillary cleared her throat uncomfortably and reached for the door handle. "I'll see you tomorrow, Alex. By the way, is this formal or casual?"

"Casual. And Hillary—" he waited as she pulled the door back open to hear his comment "—I like the color of your car. Red, brassy and bold. It suits you."

Hillary slammed the door on his words and his smile. The man was impossible. And boy, was she in trouble.

Chapter Three

"No, Mother, I'm not wearing a dress. I'm wearing a pair of nice jeans and a light blue shirt with a casual blazer." Hillary held the telephone receiver slightly away from her ear as her mother launched into another discussion about clothing. "I know he's rich, Mother, but I'm not, and I can't afford to spend money on my wardrobe. Besides, I'm not out to impress the man, I'm trying to interview him." She juggled the phone as she tried to brush her hair.

"It doesn't hurt to look good, Hillary," Sandra Blaine replied. "Alexander Donovan would be a very good catch."

Hillary laughed out loud at her old-fashioned remark. "So, let someone else catch him. He's not my type."

"I don't think you have a type. You haven't dated anyone seriously in years, not since Douglas."

"I don't want to talk about Douglas."

"You never do. He and Cassie had a baby last month."

"That's nice," Hillary said evenly. "I'm very happy for them both. But if you want to work on someone about children, why don't you bother Donna? At least she's married."

"And she's trying," Sandra pointed out. "I just don't understand your reluctance to do the normal thing. All women want husbands and children and love."

"Maybe I'm not normal."

"Don't be flippant."

Hillary sighed, knowing her mother would never understand her. It had always been that way, especially after her father died. Her mother and Donna had banded together, so alike not only in looks but in feelings that she had never felt a part of their world. Even though she loved them and wanted to make them happy, she couldn't seem to stop rebelling against their ways.

"Just give the man a chance," her mother continued persuasively. "It's not like you're twenty-one anymore. You have to start thinking about your future."

"I am thinking about my future, and believe me, Alexander Donovan does not figure in it, except for the hope that this story will finally get me to where I want to be."

"Wherever that is," Sandra replied gloomily. "Oh, well, you know I love you. So be stubborn like you always are, but promise me you'll call or, better yet, come visit. I miss you."

Hillary smiled to herself, knowing that despite their differences there would always be a bond between them. "I'll try, Mom. I'm not sure about getting away, because I'll be covering Mr. Donovan until the end of September. Maybe Thanksgiving or Christmas. Try not to worry about me, okay?"

"I can't help it. You are so much like your father, impulsive and exuberant, like a hot-air balloon that just won't set down in one place. There's something to be said for building a home for yourself someplace in this world. It can be pretty lonely going it alone."

"I'm happy. I wish you would believe that."

"Maybe I will, when you really mean it."

Hillary hung up the phone feeling distinctly unsettled by her mother's words. She was happy. Her career was moving a little more slowly than she liked, but she would get there eventually. And she had lots of friends—well, a few friends anyway. There wasn't much time to form close friendships—especially with men—when she was traveling. And she would have to be pretty close to someone to open up about her past.

The thought made her feel a little guilty. Wasn't she invading Alexander Donovan's private domain? Wasn't her goal to dig deep into his personal life to find something newsworthy? She was usually able to rationalize her efforts with the thought that world leaders needed to be under scrutiny. But what about the owner of Toy Magic?

Hillary sighed as she stared into the mirror at her unruly hair. She threw down the brush and gathered her hair into a ponytail, slapping a terry-cloth tie around it to keep it in place. Then she walked out of the bedroom, rationalizing her job.

Alexander Donovan was going to be Man of the Year. He had to expect the public to be interested in him. If he wanted privacy, he should have turned down the interview. Now he was fair game, and she was a good hunter. The battle was on. He knew it as well as she did. He would throw obstacles at her, and she would deal with whatever came up. In the course of her career, she had been insulted, made fun of, avoided and most recently shot at. There wasn't anything Alex Donovan could do that would throw her off balance.

* * *

An hour later Hillary rang the doorbell to Alex's impressive Victorian mansion in the Pacific Heights district of San Francisco. He lived on a quiet street just a few blocks from San Francisco Bay. It was a far cry from her one-bedroom apartment in south San Francisco, but she didn't care. Attaining material goods had never been her first inclination. She was more interested in doing something that would influence people and the way they thought, not that this piece would do anything more than raise the blood pressure of American women everywhere. With a glum smile she pushed the button again and waited.

"Hi." Alex opened the door with a cheerful smile. "You're right on time. I like that in a woman." He paused. "But your clothes..."

"What's wrong with them?" she asked, running her hands over her jeans as his gaze traveled up and down her body.

"They might be a little casual for this crowd. I wouldn't want you to feel out of place."

"I'm used to that feeling, believe me. But since you didn't tell me where we were going—"

"Point taken. Why don't you come in?"

He held the door open for her, and Hillary walked into the cool interior, trying to concentrate on the house and not on the man. The trouble was, he looked even better in a pair of casual tan slacks and a white shirt than he had in his fine Italian suit. There was more of him showing and yet not enough. She cleared her throat into something close to a growl.

"Are you ready to do this interview?"

He raised an eyebrow at her tone. "Now you're mad because I said something about your clothes."

"I couldn't care less."

"You don't look bad, Hillary. I just know that some women can be rather cutthroat at these gatherings. I wouldn't want your feelings to be hurt."

"I can handle myself. Don't worry about me."

"Okay, I won't. Shall I show you around?"

Hillary nodded, suddenly realizing the foyer in which they were standing was quite amazing. The hardwood floors were slick and shiny, enhanced by the Oriental rug that lent color to the room. An enormous staircase curved from the first floor up to the second. Despite her resolve to be unaffected by his wealth, she had to admit that money did make a difference. The banister looked so slick she was tempted to ask him for a ride.

"What do you think?" Alex asked, taking in her expression. "A friend of mine is an interior decorator."

"It's beautiful," she admitted. She walked over and ran a hand along the smoothly polished banister.

"Would you like to try it out? It gives quite a ride."

Hillary looked at him in disbelief, unable to believe he had read her thoughts so easily. "You haven't?"

He shrugged. "I make toys. I'm a kid at heart. Are you sure you don't want to give it a try? Come on, you like to live dangerously, don't you?"

"Not that dangerously." Actually the idea appealed to her offbeat sense of humor, but she didn't feel like letting him in on the joke. He had no way of knowing that she made a habit out of breaking rules. He also had no way of knowing that such a habit usually got her into big trouble, and she was beginning to realize that discretion and restraint had a place in her life.

Alex shook his head in regret. "You're too serious, Miss Blaine. Life is too short to waste an opportunity such as this."

"Thanks anyway, but I can live without that thrill." She walked away from the staircase and paused in front of a painting. She wasn't an art expert by any stretch of the imagination, but she did recognize talent when she saw it. Of course, it was easy to buy talent if you had enough money. She moved out of the foyer and stood in the entryway to the living room. Another incredible masterpiece of decor greeted her eyes.

"Have you lived here long, Alex?"

"About five years. I moved in just after our Tiny Dancer doll sold out at Christmas. I'll give you a house tour when we get back, but we really should be going."

"Going where?"

"To a small party some friends of mine are throwing."

"At some point, the two of us are going to have to sit down and talk privately."

"Of course. There will be plenty of time for that." He paused as his gaze drifted to the antique clock on the mantel. "I did want to make one quick call. Do you mind?"

Hillary shrugged. "I'm on your schedule today." She walked into the living room, taking a closer look at the furniture and the paintings. The room was quite clearly an interior designer's dream. Everything matched from the flowers in the vase on the grand piano to the floral print on the wallpaper. But where was the life, the warmth?

Alex said he was a kid at heart, but this was a grown-up room with no toys. She wondered if he ever sat on the straight-back chairs or antique sofas. Somehow she didn't think so. This was just another part of the facade. There had to be a room in the house that would tell her something about him. But where?

The question persisted in her mind as she walked into the formal dining room and finally into the highly sophisticated and modern kitchen. There wasn't even a damn cereal bowl in the sink, she thought crossly. Was this guy for real?

"Here you are," Alex said, walking into the kitchen. His green eyes were laughing at her as she colored guiltily. "Find anything interesting?"

"No, but you were probably counting on that. Do you really live here or did you just rent this house for the interview?"

Alex smiled. "I live here, but some things you have to work for. Are you done? Or do you need a few more minutes to snoop?"

"I'm done—for now. Tell me, Alex. Do you have a maid?"

"A cleaning service comes in twice a week."

"I see. What about a gardener?"

"Once a week."

"Personal secretary?"

"Rosemary handles all of my business."

"What about your laundry? Who does that?"

He smiled at her demanding tone. "I send it out. Actually, the service picks it up."

She nodded grimly. "All the luxuries of life. It must be nice." She preceded him out of the kitchen and down the hall to the entryway. Her movements were quick and sharp, matching the restlessness in her soul. Her second day on the job and she was already feeling irritated.

Alex put a hand on her shoulder as she reached for the door. She sent him a sharp look. "What?"

"Did I pass?"

"I don't know what you mean."

"Your questions? Did I give you the right answers?" He put his hands on her arms, but she stepped back, shrugging them off. It was hard enough to think when he wasn't touching her or looking at her with that quirky smile.

She shook her head. "There are no right answers. I'm just trying to learn what I can about you. Even the most inconsequential things can be important to the overall picture."

"Like my laundry?" he said skeptically.

"Exactly. For instance, if you had a penchant for separating colors and whites, it would say something about the orderliness of your mind, your precise thinking."

"So I've disappointed you."

His eyes were suddenly too perceptive, and he was standing so close she could smell the hint of lemon in his after-shave, see the traces of beard along his jawline. Her heart started beating faster, and she was struck by the intensity of her reaction to him. This was not going to work. She needed to keep her objectivity, to study him like an ant under a microscope, not get caught up in verbal sparring.

"Didn't you say we had a party to go to?" she asked.

"Ah, evasion. Nice move." Alex clapped his hands in mocking applause as she turned to the door. "At least we have one thing in common, Hillary. We both like our privacy. I hope you'll remember that."

"Where is this party?" Hillary asked, attempting to change the subject.

"On a boat in the marina. Let's go." He picked up his keys from a side table and gave her a gentle push through the front door, then turned to lock it behind him. When he started to move down the steps toward the driveway, Hillary remained motionless. He was almost at his car when he looked back at her in surprise. "What's the matter?"

Hillary swallowed hard. "Did you say 'boat'?"

"Yes. Come on, we're going to be late."

Hillary hesitated, memories of a fateful fourth-grade fishing trip going through her mind.

"Is there a problem? I thought you were the reporter that could handle anything? Sailing is a wonderful sport. In fact, it's a passion with me."

At any other time she would have had a quick comeback for the word "passion," especially when he drawled the word out with a sexy smile, but she was so caught up in the idea of getting on a boat that she couldn't do anything more than nod. It took all her willpower to move her feet slowly down the drive. If she didn't get on the boat, she would miss a perfect opportunity to interview him, and he might even complain to Roger that she couldn't handle the assignment. All she needed now was to get kicked off this story. That would surely send her career to an all-time low.

Look on the positive side, she told herself as she got into the car. She wasn't ten years old anymore, maybe things had changed. Sailing in a yacht was probably nothing like going out in a small fishing boat.

Two hours later she knew it was worse. The yacht was cruising under the Golden Gate Bridge, bouncing in the waves as the wind lifted it up only to smash it down again in glee, like a two-year-old playing with a toy ship.

The first hour had been fine. The party of twenty had remained docked at the pier with several waiters passing out appetizers and champagne. Then they had sailed out into the bay, gliding slowly along the shoreline, taking a good view of Alcatraz Island before heading out for turbulent waters.

A splash of ocean spray hit her in the face as the boat came down at a particularly vicious angle, and she held on to the side in a death grip. She had come out on deck be-

cause the motion had seemed even worse in the main
cabin, although everyone else seemed to be able to maintain their balance while drinking champagne and sinking
tiny pieces of French bread into a cheese fondue.

The thought of the food below turned her stomach over,
and she prayed for relief.

"Hillary. You look absolutely..." Alex paused by her
side, studying her face with genuine concern. "You're
green. I've heard people described that way, but I've never
actually seen it before."

"Thanks for the update." She pushed the hair out of her
face, but the wind whipped it back across her eyes. Somehow the wind had loosened her ponytail, and she couldn't
let go of the side long enough to look for the terry-cloth tie.

"Maybe some food," Alex suggested.

"No!" she exclaimed. "Don't even mention that word
to me."

"Sorry." He put an arm around her shoulders, steadying her as the boat rocked back and forth. "It's rougher
than usual today."

"It doesn't matter. I used to get seasick when I was little. I haven't been on a boat in years."

"Why didn't you tell me?"

She sent him an irritated look. "Following you around
is my job."

"Not to the point where you have to get sick. This is my
fault for challenging you back at the house. I didn't think.
You seemed so tough, so capable of handling anything. It's
nice to know you have a soft spot."

"I am tough," she replied shakily, helplessly steadying
herself against his arm as the boat took another dive. "I'll
be fine. I just need some air."

He smiled. "There's plenty of that out here. You know, for someone who wants to know all my deep, dark secrets, you certainly seem to have a few of your own."

"But I'm not going to be Man of the Year."

"Right. I guess that makes everything okay, at least in your mind. Don't you ever have doubts about what you're doing, the impact your stories might have on someone's life?"

She blinked back a spray of salty water from her eyes, trying to concentrate on his words, but the rocking of the boat and the motion of her stomach made coherent thought impossible. "I'm a reporter. I don't make the news, I report it. If you can't stand the heat, get out of the kitchen."

He laughed. "Or get off the boat, as the case may be."

She glared at him, not amused by the analogy.

Alex leaned back against the rail. "What do you want to ask me? I promised you some time, and we seem to be the only two out here. Fire away."

Hillary looked at him in amazement. His only conceding point to the rough seas was one hand braced against a pole. "You want to talk now?"

"It's up to you. I'm here. You're the one who has been complaining that I don't want to do the interview. You now have my undivided attention."

His complacent smile sent her temper to the breaking point. "That's just great. You finally have a chance to talk, and I can't think about anything but keeping those little red strawberries down in my stomach," she shouted. "I tried to speak to you earlier, and all I got to do was chit-chat with your high-society friends, who couldn't wait to find out if I'd tested your sexual prowess, and who, by the way, don't seem to have any more substance than you do.

I'm not even sure at this point if you're human enough to be Man of the Year.''

"Oh, I'm human all right." He straightened and took a step closer to her. "As for sexual prowess, I'm man enough to want to kiss you even though you look like you might throw up all over my shoes."

"All over your three-hundred-dollar tennis shoes."

"What? You don't like them?" He took another step closer, challenging her with his eyes.

"I hate them. They're too much. Just like everything I've seen about you is too much. You have people to cater to your every whim. My God, you probably even have someone to tie those shoes for you."

"But no one to kiss me," he said, lowering his head to brush his lips against her forehead.

"Don't do that." She put a hand up as she took a step backward. "You have plenty of women inside who would love to be with you."

"But I don't want them."

"Why not?"

"Because they say all the right things and wear the right clothes and wouldn't dream of getting seasick on a luxury yacht in the middle of a party. Whereas you are like a breath of all this fresh air out here."

"I'm not interested," she said. "So just keep your hands and everything else to yourself."

"Why? What's the worst that could happen? You already dislike me."

"I could write a horrible article about you."

He smiled gently. "You could do that anyway."

Hillary shook her head, disliking the intent gleam in his eyes. "I'm not like those other people in the cabin down there. I don't give a damn about your toy company or whether you made a couple of million last year. All I want is a good story." She made another futile attempt to get her hair out of her face. "And I look like hell right now, so don't try to pretend you're interested in me and that you aren't playing some kind of crazy game."

His smile widened into a grin. "I've always loved a good game. But you're wrong about one thing, you don't look like hell, far from it. You look alive and vibrant, like a woman who could kiss me without worrying about her lipstick." He lowered his head, his lips caressing her cheek.

She ducked under his arm, breathing hard. She had to put some space between them. "I'm not your challenge. So get that out of your head. I'm going to do my job. That's it. This story is important to me. I am not going to mess it up by getting involved with you."

"No." Alex shook his head decisively. "You're a realist, Hillary. You can't ignore the fact that there is an attraction between us. I felt it almost immediately. I'm sure you did, too."

"Don't be ridiculous. We're complete opposites. You want to play games, and I want to make changes in the world."

"Why don't you start by making a change in my world?" he challenged. "You can't lie to me, Hillary, and you can't lie to yourself. We're attracted to each other. That's nothing to be ashamed of. We're two adults. We can make our own choices."

His voice filled with intensity, matching the turbulent motion of the sea and her stomach. She couldn't think straight anymore. He was saying things she didn't want to hear.

The wind blew salt against her lips, and she reached out her tongue to wipe it away. She saw his eyes follow her movement and for a moment she was tempted to ask him to do it for her.

He must have read her mind, because he stepped forward, his eyes as green as the sea. "Give in, Hillary. You can't fight both of us."

"Never."

The defiant word echoed between them. Alex took a step forward and Hillary took a step back, wondering if she could really say no.

"It's only a matter of time."

"Don't be so sure, Alex. I can be very stubborn."

"So can I."

He took a step forward, and she took a step back, coming up against the side of the boat. There was nowhere else to run. She put a hand to ward him off. He wrapped his fingers around hers and pulled her closer.

"This isn't about the story, Hillary. This is about you and me, a man and a woman, who don't have to pretend with each other. Give in."

She wanted to say yes, but the predatory gleam in his eyes made her realize how much he wanted from her. It wouldn't be a simple kiss. It would be a turning point, and she wasn't ready. Not here, not now, not on a boat that made her stomach do somersaults. It could jeopardize everything else in her life. But if she didn't say something, he was going to kiss her, and she was going to let him.

"Alex, please . . ." Her voice trailed off as she was once again caught in his gaze. It was too late. She couldn't say no. She didn't want to say no.

He put his hands on her waist and pulled her body up against him, his gaze never leaving her face. He bent his head to kiss her lips when the ocean answered her silent call for help. A large wave hit the boat hard, sending water pouring over the side, spraying them both with a vengeance.

Hillary gasped, the shock of the cold water driving everything else from her mind. She looked at Alex, and he looked back, his eyes echoing her own shock. She was so confused, she didn't know whether to yell or scream or throw up.

Alex solved the problem by breaking into a chuckle that soon grew into a full-blown laugh. It was contagious in its appeal, and her reluctant smile blossomed into a wide grin. They were both dripping wet and freezing cold, but for once Alexander Donovan looked like a real person and not a programmed robot. Darn, if he wasn't more appealing.

Alex continued to laugh as he brushed water out of his face. "That's one for you, Hillary, but the battle is far from over. You can quote me on that."

Chapter Four

An hour later Hillary slipped into the front seat of Alex's Mercedes and breathed a sigh of relief. Her stomach was still churning, and her legs felt as though they might give out at any moment, but at least she was off the boat, on dry land and away from the smirking smiles of Alex's so-called friends.

Of course she was also wet and clammy with goose bumps down her arms growing more pronounced by each sway of the afternoon breeze. Her interview with Alex was certainly off to a good start. Yesterday she had walked in on the middle of his insulting remarks, bristled back in impulsive defense, and today she had narrowly avoided throwing up all over him.

She didn't even want to begin to think about his flirting comments. That was an area that was better addressed when she was home alone and able to reshore her defenses against his easy charm.

Alex pulled the car out of the marina parking lot and paused at the light leading onto Bay Street. Hillary sighed at the wait, eager to put the yachting trip behind her.

In response, Alex reached out and patted a hand on her leg. "We'll be home soon. How are you feeling?"

"Just peachy, thanks."

Alex smiled at her sharp retort and eased the car onto the street as the light turned green. "You're a terrible liar. You don't look peachy. In fact, you look pretty pale. The green has turned into a grayish white."

"I know I look awful. You don't have to rub it in."

"Sorry." He patted her leg again, realizing she was soaked through her blue jeans. "I think you need a change of clothes."

"I'm fine. I can live with being a little wet."

"I know you can. You're one tough lady."

"You make it sound like an insult."

His head tipped to one side in thoughtful deliberation. "I didn't mean it that way. Actually, I'm very impressed with your resiliency. I know you didn't feel well back there, but you didn't do anything to draw attention to yourself. Nor did you ask for help. Although, I think you may have too much pride for your own good."

"Since we've only known each other a little over twenty-four hours, I hardly think you're qualified to make a statement like that."

Alex smiled but didn't say anything, and Hillary leaned back against the seat. The fact that his words were so close to the mark was a little unsettling. He seemed to be able to see right through her or at least into the tiny recesses of her mind that no one else had been able to bridge.

This was not going to work. He was the subject. She was the interviewer, not the other way around, but somehow he kept turning the tables on her.

Once again she was filled with the longing to toss the assignment back to Roger with a "thanks, but no thanks," and hop on a plane for some foreign, exotic city where she could sink her teeth into a news story that didn't involve an exciting, sexy, complicated man. A couple of flirtatious lines, a quirky smile, and she had been ready to throw herself into his arms and forget about everything else. Alex Donovan was more dangerous than a loaded gun.

She had to get away from him, find some breathing room and get her head back together. Unfortunately she had a story to do, an interview piece that could make or break her job. She had to concentrate on that purpose and push everything else out of her mind. She had to ask sharp, penetrating questions, get good, interesting answers and then put the story to bed. *Or put Alex to bed.* Good Lord, what was she thinking? Frowning, she shook her head, trying to clear her mind.

"Something wrong?" Alex asked curiously. "You seem to be wrestling with yourself."

She flung him a quick look, marveling again at his perception. It was time to retake control of the situation. "When we get back to your house, I think we should talk, get this interview rolling." Alex started to refuse even before she finished her statement. "Why not?"

"Because I have another appointment. We can meet tonight when I take you to the cocktail reception for the mayor."

Hillary gritted her teeth, trying to hang on to her patience. "We won't be able to talk at a party. Isn't there any way you can postpone what you're doing this afternoon?"

"Sorry, it's business."

"You aren't going to make this easy for me, are you?"

"Do you really want me to?"

"No, of course not. I enjoy ramming my head against a brick wall."

Alex burst out laughing. "I've never met anyone who says exactly what they think. You are one of a kind, Miss Blaine."

"I wish I could return the compliment, but I don't know who you are, and you seem determined to keep me in the dark."

His expression quieted, the amusement fading from his green eyes. "Maybe it's better that way."

"Why? Do you have something to hide?"

"No, of course not."

"Of course not," she echoed, not believing him for one second.

"I'm just a man, probably not worth making Man of the Year, but then that was your magazine's choice, not mine. If I don't measure up in your eyes, maybe you should go back to your boss and ask for someone else." He gave her a sharp, knowing look and then directed his attention back to the traffic.

Hillary stared out the window at the cars and a passing trio of bicyclists enjoying a carefree day. It would be nice to get out of this assignment, but she knew Roger wouldn't change his opinion about Alex Donovan, and she also knew she couldn't give up a cover story without suffering the consequences. Alex thought she had too much pride, but not this time. She would do whatever it took to get the job done and move up on the career ladder.

"I don't know if you measure up," she said. "Because so far we haven't gotten past the surface. The neighborhood grocer probably knows more about you than I do."

A deep, warm chuckle filled the air as Alex looked at her in amusement. "Herman knows I hate brussels sprouts, but he certainly doesn't know how I kiss, so I guess you're even."

Hillary glared at him through strands of wet blond hair, but Alex simply reached out and tucked her hair behind one ear, a tender gesture that got to her more than anything else he had done. Her tension eased, and she found herself smiling back. "You're trouble, Donovan. I should have figured that from the beginning. After all, you can't get to be a playboy without some charm."

A long pause fell between them as Alex maneuvered the car through the busy afternoon traffic. Hillary settled back in her seat, crossing her legs in the roomy interior. Now that her stomach had stopped doing somersaults, she was able to enjoy the scenery along this edge of the city. A few miles ahead were the tourist meccas of Fisherman's Wharf and Ghiradelli Square, but here by the marina, the locals were simply flying kites on the marina greens or walking along the bay, watching the wind surfers. Hillary felt a sudden lightness creep into her soul.

Alex might have his secrets, and she might have the devil of a time figuring them out, but she had to admit there was something nice about just being with him. He was exhilarating and challenging, and fun to spar with. He treated her as an equal, and his ego didn't seem to be nearly as big as she had first imagined, or else he was a very good actor.

The problem was more his sexy smile and green eyes that reflected every mood, the taut muscles of his body, and the power in his movements. He had a presence that was hard to ignore, and when he turned on the charm, he put shivers down her spine. That was the real problem. The incredible attraction insinuating itself between them, underlying every word, every casual gesture, made it difficult to keep her mind on business. She hadn't felt so wanted in a long time, if ever.

Hillary took in a deep breath and slowly let it out, trying to regain her poise. "What time is the party tonight?"

"Six o'clock. Shall I pick you up?"

"I can meet you at your house."

Alex sent her a questioning look. "You've already seen my home. I'd like to see yours."

"It's an apartment in south San Francisco not an elegant mansion. There's nothing to see."

"I'm sure it would tell me something about you, who you are, the way you like to live."

Hillary smiled at him. "Why would you think that? I didn't get even a tiny clue from your house."

"Maybe you didn't look closely enough."

"Are you going to give me another chance?"

"Of course." Alex turned down his street and pulled up to the sidewalk in front of her car, keeping the motor running. "But not today. I have that appointment to keep."

"The mysterious appointment. Is it toy business or monkey business?"

"What do you think?"

"That you're evading the question, again." Hillary opened the door, but didn't get out of her seat. "I'm not going to give up, Alex. It's my job to interview you. To come up with a bright, interesting profile on our Man of the Year. Now you can make that easy or you can make it difficult, but one way or another it is going to happen. I am not going to be put off by cocktail parties and boat trips, no matter how many times I have to throw up my breakfast."

His laugh cut her off in midstream, and she tried to retain her serious expression, but in the light of his amusement, it was a tough task to pull off. "I'm serious, Alex."

"I know you are. Okay, close your door and put your seat belt back on."

"Really?"

"Yes, because I have the feeling that if I don't take you with me, you'll simply get in your car and follow me."

Hillary gave him an innocent look as she refastened her seat belt. "Me? I'm not a spy, I'm a reporter."

"Whatever. At least you're dressed right for this place."

She looked down at her damp jeans and shirt, suddenly realizing her attire was hardly professional. Her blond hair was stringy and wet and frizzing from the sea breeze. There couldn't be an ounce of makeup left on her ocean-washed face, and her shoes made a decidedly squishy sound when she moved her legs. "You mean we're not going on another escape with the rich and famous?"

He shook his head. "Nope."

"Where are we going?"

Alex gunned the motor and pulled away from the sidewalk with a decided squeal of the tires. "To hell and back. Hang on."

It wasn't hell, but then again it probably wasn't far from it. The streets in this part of San Francisco were dark and grimy, with people loitering in the alleys and along the sidewalks. The weather was hot, the air oppressive, and Hillary began to wonder just what Alex was up to. His Mercedes came under intense scrutiny by the local passersby, and when they stopped at an intersection, she instinctively locked her door.

The motion brought Alex's gaze to her face. When she turned to look at him, his eyes were serious and intense, and she couldn't begin to imagine what had brought on such strong emotions.

"Not your kind of town, is it? Do you want me to take you home?"

"No." She forced a note of casualness into her voice. "I'm a reporter. I'm used to following stories wherever they go."

"As long as you can lock your door," he said whimsically.

"It doesn't hurt to be cautious."

"No, of course not. I just don't want to make you uncomfortable. Some people like to pretend these places don't exist."

"I would never do that, and I'm fine, Alex. Just drive." Hillary looked out the window at the dirty shop windows. The building on the corner was a dry-cleaners that had iron bars across the glass. Next door was a small restaurant boasting tacos, and down the street was a pawn shop. It was not the San Francisco of the tourist brochures, the cosmopolitan city where people like Alex Donovan wined and dined in fancy restaurants or on elegant yachts. It was an urban neighborhood suffering a harsh economic reality. She couldn't imagine where they were going. Maybe Alex was taking a shortcut. It was the only answer that made sense. What business would he have on a street like this?

He turned the car into an alley, the passageway so narrow Hillary thought she could reach out a hand and touch the buildings they were passing. Finally the alley opened up and set back to one side was a three-car parking lot and a dirty white sign that read To Hell And Back.

Alex pulled into a parking spot and cut the engine. "You thought I was kidding, didn't you?"

"What is this place?"

"Let's go in and see." He opened the car door and got out, waiting for her to join him. Then he walked over to a large warehouse door. He pushed back a heavy bolt and walked inside, pulling the door shut behind them.

Hillary blinked several times, giving her eyes a chance to adjust to the dimness after the bright light outside.

"Yo, dude. Who's the broad?"

"Woman," Alex corrected, punching the arm of a tough-looking teenager wearing shorts and a tank top. "Hillary Blaine, meet Sammy Jordan."

"Hello." Hillary extended her hand despite the boy's raised eyebrows.

Sammy took her hand reluctantly and shook it.

"What do you say?" Alex prodded.

"Excellent." The boy drew out the word with a low-key whistle at the end.

Alex laughed. "I agree, but that wasn't what I meant."

"Oh, yeah. Pleased to meet you." He turned to Alex. "What's up? You want some action tonight?"

"No, thanks. I'm looking for Micky."

The boy tilted his head back toward the main gymnasium. "In there. Later, dude." He sauntered out the door, taking one last appreciative look at Hillary's slim figure.

Hillary shifted her feet self-consciously and then flushed as Alex caught her eye.

"Better get used to it," he said. "Not too many women who look like you come in here."

"Like me?" she echoed in confusion. She looked down at her blue jeans in bewilderment. She had never thought of herself as anything but a ragged tomboy, a duck in a circle of elegant swans, and today she certainly didn't look like anything else.

"Yes, like you, gorgeous, and you don't even know what I'm talking about. Maybe that's what's so appealing," he replied, studying her with a thoughtfulness that only made her more uneasy.

She felt suddenly feminine and vulnerable, and that was the last way she wanted to feel, especially with him. "Don't be silly," she said. "I'd appreciate it if you would keep comments like that to yourself. I'm a hard-boiled journalist here to do a story, not some debutante you're trying to impress."

"Yes, sir. I mean, ma'am."

"Are we going inside, Alex?"

"After you."

Hillary walked toward the open door where the sound of grunting and pounding feet was followed by some of the foulest language she had ever heard. Instinctively she paused and then pressed forward as Alex pushed her through the opening.

Once inside, her jaw dropped in amazement. There was a boxing ring in the middle of the room with two boys sparring. Another group of teenagers was working out on weights along one wall while a lone runner ran laps around the indoor track.

"Go on," Alex encouraged. "They won't bite, at least not while I'm here."

Hillary walked into the center of the room at his urging and the feeling of self-consciousness returned after dozens of pairs of eyes followed their movements. She instinctively walked closer to Alex, feeling comforted by his presence at her side. He must have interpreted her need, because he flung a casual arm around her shoulders that for the first time that day was not followed by a flirtatious comment. Normally she would have stepped aside in independent righteousness, but it felt too good, and it seemed too harmless to make a case out of removing his arm.

"Faster, Danny. Move those feet. Dance, baby, dance." A man shouted the words at one of the struggling teenagers in the ring as Alex and Hillary looked on. A couple more jabs and then he called time out, speaking quietly to the boys before sending them to the showers.

Alex waited until he was done and then raised a hand to wave him over. "Micky."

The man nodded and slipped through the ropes on the ring. When he reached Alex, instead of offering him a polite handshake, he gave him a bear hug and slapped him hard on the back.

Hillary watched the two men with interest. Although Alex was tall and well built, Micky was positively overwhelming. Not an ounce of fat on his body, he was big, burly and strong, a blond Nordic god.

"You're late," Micky growled.

"Sorry, I got delayed."

Micky looked at Hillary and smiled, transforming his intimidating face. "So, I see. Micky Gallant, at your service," he said.

"Hillary Blaine," she replied, unable to resist his bearish charm.

"She's doing a story on me for *World Today* magazine," Alex said. "My permanent shadow for the next couple of weeks."

"Lucky you."

Alex ignored him and reached into his pocket for an envelope. "Here's the check. Don't let it go so long next time. If you need help, just call."

"You've done enough already. I hate to keep asking."

"As long as you keep getting results, that's all that matters."

Micky pointed to the ring where two older boys were pulling on boxing gloves. "I got an up-and-coming champion ready to go. Want to watch?"

Alex looked questioningly at Hillary. "How's your stomach?"

"Why? Is there going to be blood?"

"You never know. Micky doesn't pull any punches with these kids."

Hillary rolled her eyes at his pun. Shrugging out from under his protective arm, she walked closer to the ring, eager to see firsthand what was involved in training a champion.

"Rudy just got out of jail three weeks ago," Alex said quietly in her ear, motioning to the tall, thin youth preparing to begin his match. "Shoplifting food for his seven brothers and sisters."

"That's terrible."

"Yes, it is. Hopefully, he can learn a few other skills here."

"What is this place, Alex?" Hillary looked at him curiously, struck by the passion in his voice, the genuine caring that seemed to flow between him and the boys.

"It's a neighborhood gym for street kids. Micky is an ex-boxer. He medalled at the Olympics some years back. He opened this place about three years ago to get some of the kids off the street. Micky grew up in a neighborhood like this."

"And you? What do you have to do with this place? You obviously didn't grow up here."

Alex's lips tightened at her comment. "No, I didn't grow up here, but that doesn't mean I can't offer a helping hand, does it?"

"No. In fact, it makes the offer seem more generous."

"Don't make me out to be a saint. I throw a few dollars this way now and then. It's no big deal. I can afford it."

Hillary stared at his harsh profile, wondering why there seemed to be so much more behind his simple statement.

He was right, he could afford it, and certainly many wealthy businessmen invested back into the community, but this place, this gym, seemed too personal for a casual investment.

"How long have you been involved?" she asked.

"A few years. I don't keep track."

"How did you meet Micky?"

Alex smiled at her persistence. "I met Micky years ago, long before anyone wanted to make me Man of the Year."

"In school or through friends?"

"Friends." He tipped his head toward the ring. "You're going to miss the action if you keep asking questions."

"I think I'm going to miss the action if I stop," she said. "Do you care if I write about your involvement with this gym?"

"No. I'm sure the press would do them good. In fact, it might even bring in a few more investors."

"Then you don't mind if I talk to Micky?"

Alex hesitated. "He looks pretty busy today. Maybe another time."

"You're not stalling me?"

"Would I do that?"

"In a second."

Alex put his arm around her shoulders and hugged her tight to his body. "You know, it's very unsettling to be with a woman who's always trying to find out what kind of underwear you have on."

Hillary's jaw dropped at his personal reference, her thoughts echoed by a kid walking just behind them.

"She can check out my boxers anytime, man."

Alex shook a warning finger at him. "She's mine, Eddie. Back off."

Hillary pulled away from him. "I am not yours. I don't belong to anybody."

"Then I don't have any competition, do I?" Alex laughed at her irritation. "Relax. I'm just teasing you. I know you have a sense of humor, even if you do try to cover it up. In fact, I bet you're just dying to smile at me right now."

Hillary pursed her lips, determined not to give in. "I'm not amused."

"Good grief. Now you sound like the Queen of England."

"Would you stop? I'm trying to watch a boxing match. I want to see how your friend Micky works. He's obviously an expert."

"At boxing, yes. But you don't care about that. You just can't wait to get to him and give him the third degree." He leaned closer to whisper in her ear. "But even he doesn't know what kind of underwear I have on. Some things you have to find out for yourself."

Hillary let out a sigh and relaxed her lips. There was no point in trying to be serious when he was determined to make her smile. "Maybe so. But he's the first friend of yours who seems to have more depth than a champagne bubble. So, if you have nothing to hide, I'm sure you won't mind if I talk to him."

Alex ran a hand through his hair. "Of course not," he said. *As long as I can get to him first.*

Chapter Five

It was nearly four o'clock when Alex walked back into the gym. He had dropped Hillary at her car, waited to make sure she was heading toward home, and then retraced his steps. A new set of boys was filling the gym for Saturday-night sparring, an event he sometimes liked to watch to keep up with the potential new talent. If Micky found someone with determination and courage and a willingness to work, Alex would slide a little extra money in that direction, give the kid a boost. But today he had more on his mind than the kids and their boxing dreams.

Her name was Hillary, and she was a sexy blonde with an attitude. The more he saw of her, the more chaos she created in his life. It had seemed so simple in the beginning. Set up an interview, take the reporter to the right social events, bore her to tears and then get rid of her. But it wasn't working that way. She wasn't following the game plan, and her unpredictability was making him forget some of the rules.

He should never have brought her to the gym. Maybe she would have found out about it eventually, but the location might have daunted her from venturing in on her own. Even as the thought crossed his mind, he realized how silly it was. Hillary wouldn't let a simple thing like a neighborhood get in her way. She was too tough. He smiled to himself. She was also exquisitely soft in just the right places.

With a shake of his head and a reminder to stay focused, he walked down the hall to Micky's office and pounded on the door. "Did you forget something?" Micky asked in surprise. "Or did you just miss my sweet face?"

Alex walked in and shut the door behind him. "We need to talk."

"In a second." Micky punched out numbers on a calculator, adding up a string of invoices, and then swore softly. "We're over budget again. The entries in the San Jose Boxing Competition ran high this year."

"How much?"

"Seventy-five bucks."

Alex rolled his eyes and dug into his pocket for his wallet. "You want it in twenties or tens?"

"I'll take it in quarters. But you shouldn't be walking around with that much cash." He motioned toward the wad in Alex's hand. "People like you get robbed down here."

"People like me know how to protect themselves."

Micky took the money and counted it out. "Thanks. Now what's on your mind, the good-looking reporter?" He looked around inquiringly. "Where is she, anyway?"

"I hope she's at home, but you never know."

Alex picked up a pile of T-shirts off the chair in front of the desk and tossed them onto the floor. "This place is a mess." He waved a hand toward a pile of folders on one corner of the desk, three half-filled cups of coffee and a stack of boxing magazines. "Don't you ever clean up?"

"Not too often. So hire me a cleaning lady and get off my case. Now, talk. I have a lot of work to do before we start the matches tonight."

Alex sighed as he sat back in his chair, folding his arms in front of his chest. He didn't know why he'd come running back to the gym. The rationalization that he needed to warn Micky seemed a little foolish in retrospect. Micky could take care of himself. God knows he'd been doing it long enough, just as he had. They were both street smart and certainly too savvy to say anything foolish to a reporter.

"I don't have all day," Micky reminded him. "Are you going to talk? Or should I come back in an hour?"

"I may have a problem," Alex said finally.

Micky laughed. "I think you definitely have a problem, and her name is Hillary."

"Yes, but not in the way you mean." Alex frowned at the cheerful expression on Micky's face. "She's doing a story on me."

"That's not all she's doing on you."

"I'm talking about my past. Hillary is going to try to talk to you. In fact, I was almost afraid I'd run into her on my way back here."

"And you want me to cover for you?" Micky leaned back in his chair and kicked his feet up on the desk. "I don't know if I should."

"What does that mean?"

"It means that I think the lady might be good for you, but not if you don't come clean."

"I'm not talking about a date here, Micky. I'm talking about a woman who could destroy me and a few other people with an article that says too much."

"Then why did you agree to the interview?"

"Because I was a fool," Alex shouted in frustration, running a hand through his hair. "Okay. Are you satisfied?"

"No, I'm not." Micky leaned forward, an intent look on his face. "We go back a long way, longer than we'd both like to remember, and I'm almost insulted that you felt it necessary to come back here and warn me not to talk." He held up a hand as Alex started to interrupt. "But I can understand that this woman seems to be making you a little crazy, so I'll let it go."

"Good," Alex said with relief. "You don't have to lie. You just don't have to add anything to whatever she asks you. I said we met through mutual friends, which is basically the truth."

"Basically. What makes you think she's going to talk to me?"

"Because she was practially drooling at the thought of getting something juicy on me, and you seem like her best prospect. She is stubborn and determined, so I know she'll be back."

"She's also easy on the eyes. How come the only reporters I see are forty-five and balding?"

"Just lucky I guess." Alex rocked the chair back on its hind legs.

"Don't do that, you'll break the chair."

Alex rolled his eyes again and set it down with a bang. "Yes, Mother."

"Someone has to keep you in line." Micky stood up and stretched his arms high above his head. "You know, I think you ought to give this woman a chance to be something more than professional. I saw the way you were looking at her."

"She's not for me," Alex said, although silently he admitted the truth. He was interested in Hillary. He felt exhilarated by her presence, charged by her sharp wit and touched by the vulnerability he sometimes saw in her eyes. He wanted to see her smile and laugh, to feel her appreciation and respect not just her skepticism.

It was crazy, wanting to impress her. But deep down he knew that was why he'd brought her to the gym. He was tired of the pretense he was showing her, the sophisticated man, the worldly jet-setter. He wanted her to know that there was more to him than she thought. And he'd done just that. Now she was doubly curious and he was in bigger trouble than before.

Micky tossed a pencil down on the desk, the noise breaking through Alex's thoughts. "She has a hell of a lot more going for her than those skinny models you hang out with."

Alex nodded reluctantly. "Maybe so, but those women are not interested in finding out any more about me than the size of my wallet, the make of my car, and the extent of my generosity. I can handle that. There are no ties, no commitments. Everyone has a good time and then we say goodbye."

"And no one gets close. I hear you, Alex. I've felt the same way myself. But one of these days, I'm afraid you're going to meet a woman who won't walk away that easily." Micky paused for a long moment, as they each got caught up in their own thoughts. Finally he broke the silence. "What happens if she does find something out? What then?"

Alex's mouth tightened into a grim line, and he felt his shoulders stiffen at the thought. He'd have only one option, and there wouldn't be any other choice, no matter what his feelings about Hillary. "I'd have to make sure she didn't use it."

"By doing what?"

"Whatever I have to."

Micky nodded. "Maybe when Hillary gets here, I should offer her some boxing gloves. She might need them before you're through."

Hillary was wrestling with a stubborn zipper on the back of her emerald green cocktail dress when the doorbell rang. Swearing under her breath, she gave the zipper another impatient tug, glaring at her expression in the mirror. The dress clung to her body like a second skin, and her blond hair tumbled around her shoulders in a mass of curls from a last-minute roll up.

This was not her. Who was she kidding? She looked downright sexy. Definitely not the image she wanted to portray around Alexander Donovan. She had to change, smooth out her hair, take off the bright lipstick and not try to be something she wasn't just because some stupid man had gotten her blood pressure up.

The doorbell rang again, reminding her that there was no time for second thoughts. With one arm holding the back of her dress together, she stalked to the front door and threw it open, glaring at the man on the doorstep.

"You're early," she said.

Alex raised one eyebrow and then consulted his gold Rolex watch. "Five minutes late, actually."

She let out a heavy sigh and stood back. "You might as well come in."

"Thank you."

"You're welcome." Hillary pulled restlessly on the zipper as she turned to go back into her bedroom, but it wouldn't move. She would simply go into her room, take out a pair of scissors and cut the damn thing in two. But Alex caught her around the waist, pulling her back against his chest before she could speak or even breathe for that matter.

"Looks like you have a problem," he said, his breath fanning the side of her face.

"I'm fine." Her voice came out jerky, the movement of his hand across her midriff making her distinctly uneasy.

"Too stubborn to ask for help?"

"I can do it myself. Just let me go."

"If you don't want half the men in San Francisco to see your naked back, you'll let me help. Although, this isn't a bad view." He lowered his head and kissed the side of her neck, sending a nervous tingle down her spine. She could almost imagine his lips blazing the same trail her zipper normally took.

"You have beautiful skin."

"I have freckles on my shoulders," Hillary said deliberately, trying to break the subtle mood of intimacy that always seemed to envelop them. "If you want to help, why don't you fix the zipper?"

"I thought you'd never ask."

Hillary stared straight ahead while Alex took a look at the problem. If she stared hard enough at the long crack of plaster in the wall, maybe she would forget he was even there. But the wall didn't do it for her, so she turned her gaze to the coffee table, wincing at the layer of dust under the magazines. Lord, she even had a pile of laundry on the chair that she had meant to take downstairs to wash. Her apartment was nowhere near the pristine clean of Alex's house.

Oh well, creative minds often expressed themselves better in creative surroundings. She smiled at her own rationalization, trying to think about anything but the touch of his fingers against her bare skin.

She had wanted to get away from him, not press her half-naked body against his chest and wish that he would pull the zipper down instead of up. But as usual, things hadn't turned out quite the way she'd planned.

"You've got yourself in quite a pickle," Alex said, tugging at the zipper as he played with the cloth blocking its way.

"You can say that again."

"What?"

"Nothing." Hillary shivered under his touch, feeling a reckless yearning take over her mind and body. She wanted to lean back against him, to feel his arms slide all the way around her waist. He would lower his head and his lips would touch the side of her neck. He would call her beautiful and sexy in that deep, baritone voice. Then she would turn and—

"It's stuck," Alex said bluntly, disrupting her fantasy like a burst of cold water.

She straightened her shoulders. "I know it's stuck. If you'll let me go, I'll just get some scissors and—"

"No way. I'm not going to let you destroy this dress. It's gorgeous." Alex worked at the material with his fingers. "You're too impatient, Hillary. Don't you know the best things take time?" The last few words were said quietly, almost sensuously near the side of her ear, and she knew he wasn't talking about her zipper anymore.

She turned her head to look at the wall over her dining room table. Fortunately she was staring straight at her display of press clippings. The award-winning stories her father had written were framed and lovingly placed in the center of the wall. They reminded her of what was important. They were her inspiration, her focus in life. She had to stop acting like a woman around Alex and start acting like a reporter.

"I think I've got it." With a sigh of satisfaction, Alex pulled the zipper up the length of her back. "You're all set."

Hillary immediately stepped away from him, eager to get some breathing space. Without turning around, she fled into her bedroom, mumbling that she would be with him in a few minutes. When she got into the privacy of her room, she took several deep, calming breaths. She put her hands to her face, feeling the heat that was rampaging through her body despite her best intentions.

She was not going to be able to do her job if she let herself get turned on by the simple touch of his hand on her back. Walking purposefully to her dressing table, she took out her brush and ran it briskly through her hair, reaching for a gold barrette to pull it back out of her face. Her hand paused when a knock came at her door.

"Hillary? Don't put up your hair, okay?"

She didn't answer, caught between wanting to please him and wanting to be safe. Pleasure finally won out. They were going to a cocktail party, after all. Since she already had the silly dress on, she might as well go the rest of the way.

When she returned to the living room, Alex was standing in front of her bookshelves, examining the titles with open curiosity.

"Find anything you like?" she asked.

He held up a heavy, dark brown book that dissected World War II into fifty-six chapters. "Do you have insomnia? Because if so . . ."

"That's a very interesting book. Maybe you should read it."

"I probably should. But I'm not going to pretend an interest in doing so."

Her eyes sparkled at the honest confession. "Actually that was my father's. I've never gotten past chapter four."

"What about the other military books?"

"All his. He loved spy stories. If he hadn't been such a good foreign correspondent, I think he might have joined the CIA. As it was, he was quite a legend in the newspaper business. I'm not sure I can ever reach his level." Her voice cracked with emotion. "Sorry, I get a little carried away when I think about him. He died when I was fourteen. You'd think I'd be over it by now."

"Some things you never get over," Alex said, as a strong current of understanding flowed between them.

"That's right. You lost both your parents. That must have been even worse. At least I still have my mom and my sister, although sometimes I think we live on different planets." Hillary blinked back the unexpected moisture in her eyes and tried to laugh. "I can't believe I'm telling you all this. You're the one who is supposed to be interviewed."

"I'm sure my time will come." Alex slipped the book back onto the shelf, giving Hillary a chance to regain her poise. "Where do your mom and sister live? Here in San Francisco?"

"No. My mom lives in Pasadena, that's where I grew up. My sister, Donna, lives in Arcadia, which is just a few miles from my mother. She's married and is trying to get pregnant." She waved her hand into the air. "Now you know the whole family story."

Alex smiled. "I don't think so. But it's a start. Are you ready to go?"

"Yes."

"Good, because we're late."

"Isn't that fashionable?" she asked tartly, opening the door for him so she could turn the dead bolt with her key.

"Yes, but sometimes they run out of food, and I'm starving."

There was plenty of food at the reception, Hillary thought dismally as she juggled her empty plate with her glass of champagne. There were also plenty of people and lots of loud music reverberating through the grand ballroom of the Sterling Hotel. Definitely not a place to try to have an intimate conversation with anyone, especially Mr. Popularity.

As usual, the Man of the Year was surrounded by people, and Hillary could understand why. Alex was good-looking and rich, but aside from that he was also a charismatic person who seemed to be able to change his personality and conversation to suit the person he was talking to. With the men he would trade sporting news, reciting statistics that would put most baseball fans to shame. With business associates, the conversation would turn to stocks and economic trends. With personal friends, Alex would change accordingly. The man was smooth, Hillary thought. If it was an act, it was definitely well rehearsed.

It was also about time she made her entrance.

After putting down her plate and glass on an empty tray, she moved through the crowd, smiling at some of the other press people present. She would have felt a lot better about the party if she had come to interview the mayor or some of the supervisors, not follow around San Francisco's most eligible bachelor. When she reached the group surrounding Alex, she jostled into a front position, waiting for a chance to break into the conversation. It was about time Alex remembered she was here, and if that meant shaking him up a little in front of his friends, so be it. She was getting tired of being pushed into the background.

Finally, she was next to Alex and with a gentle push of her elbow, she managed to dislodge a clingy redhead from his right side. She put a hand on Alex's arm and stood on tiptoe to whisper in his ear, "I'm back."

Alex didn't acknowledge the comment, but she could see a small smile play across his lips. She moved a little farther forward, so she could see exactly who he was talking to. The crowd shifted at her movement, and suddenly she was face to face with a man she had hoped she would never see again, Douglas Wilmington. She blinked, hoping the horrible mirage would disappear, but he was smiling down at her with his perfect white teeth and his beach-boy looks. Her stomach took a nosedive, and she grabbed on to Alex's arm as if he were a buoy and she was about to drown.

"Hillary?" Alex looked down at her in surprise, and the conversation around them suddenly lagged.

Her throat was too tight to reply, and she couldn't seem to stop staring at Douglas. Why him? Why now? She hated the way he made her feel, insecure and not good enough.

"Hillary? I thought that was you." This time it was Douglas who spoke her name, confident and full of himself as if she would be glad to see the man who had made a fool out of her.

"You two know each other?" Alex asked quietly.

Hillary nodded. "Yes."

"We used to be very good friends, didn't we, Hillary?"

A couple of knowing smiles broke out in the group, the same as they had the last time she'd seen Douglas at a party similar to this one. Instinctively, Hillary took a step closer to Alex, pressing against his side, hoping she could somehow share some of his strength and power.

Alex reciprocated by casually sliding an arm around her waist, making it clear that she was with him. Of course, it created a wrong impression. Now people would think she belonged to Alex, but at least it was better than them knowing her history with Douglas.

"Maybe you and Wilmington can talk later, Hillary, but right now I was thinking about attacking the buffet table, and I could use some company," Alex said. "What do you say?"

She nodded, smiling a grateful thank-you.

"If you'll excuse us," Alex said to the group as various people nodded their heads.

"I'd like to talk to you before you leave," Douglas Wilmington said. "Don't run off, okay?"

Hillary tipped her head in his direction. "Fine," she ground out, pleased that she had at least gotten her mouth to move. She hated the way she was responding to him. She wasn't the same girl she had been with Douglas, and she wished she could show him that she didn't give a damn about him anymore.

"We can talk about the old times in my apartment," Doug added, drawing a chuckle from a nearby man.

Alex started to lead her away, but Hillary hung back, looking into Douglas's smug, smiling expression. A sudden itch to slap that look off his face swept through her, so compelling she felt the fingers of her right hand clench into a fist. She even went so far as to move her arm, but Alex's hand clamped down on her shoulder.

"Time to eat, Hillary," he said firmly, drawing her away from the interested crowd. He led her through the party at a brisk pace, not stopping until they had reached the far end of the room.

"Would you let me go? People are staring at us," Hillary complained.

"They would have been looking a lot harder if I'd let you deck Douglas Wilmington."

Hillary looked at him in surprise. He seemed to be able to read her so well and yet they barely knew each other. But there was something between them so strong, so connecting, that she couldn't seem to escape it. She saw an answering gleam in his eyes and everything else faded from the scene. It wasn't Douglas that bothered her anymore, it was a sudden overwhelming feeling for Alex that filled her with panic.

Hillary stopped a passing waiter carrying a tray of champagne. She grabbed a glass and drained the liquid in one long gulp. It wasn't until she was finished that she realized Alex had done the same thing.

They stared at each other over the rims of their empty glasses, and the heat turned to humor. Alex was the first to smile, and Hillary followed reluctantly.

"I guess we were both more thirsty than hungry," she said.

"And we needed to cool down. I could use some air. Ready to go?"

"More than ready."

By the time they walked through the front doors of the hotel, Hillary was feeling more like herself. She was grateful for Alex's silence as they waited for the valet to retrieve the car, but she knew that once inside there were going to be questions, and she better have some answers—the right answers.

To his credit, Alex waited a long time. Hillary was beginning to think he was just going to let it drop until he bypassed the exit for her house and continued down the San Francisco Peninsula.

"Where are we going?" she asked.

"Somewhere we can talk, away from the crowds."

"Really? This must be my lucky night. I actually get to spend some time alone with you."

Alex didn't smile. "We're not going to talk about me, Hillary. We're going to talk about you."

"I don't have anything to say."

"We'll see." He maneuvered the car off the freeway and down a frontage road that ran along the San Francisco airport. He bypassed the trail of parking lots leading into the various hotels and didn't stop until he reached a dirt lot off to the side of the road. It was at the end of the runway, completely dark save for the lights of the planes waiting to take off.

Alex cut the engine and turned to face her, his expression grim and unyielding. Her stomach clenched. "What?"

"There's something I have to ask you, Hillary. Were you and Wilmington lovers?"

Chapter Six

Hillary swallowed hard, the question setting her teeth on edge, even though she had known all along it would be coming. "I don't think that's any of your business."

"Let's just say I'm making it my business."

"You don't have any right to ask me such a personal question." Hillary shifted so close to the door she could feel the handle jabbing into her side. If they'd been anywhere except on a deserted road at nine o'clock at night, she would have gotten out and walked away.

Alex drummed his fingers on the steering wheel. "You looked absolutely terrified when you saw him, like a ghost had suddenly risen up from a grave. I could feel you shaking, and we weren't even touching. I'm concerned." He looked at her then, waiting until she met his gaze. "I can be a good listener."

"I'm fine, Alex."

"Now, maybe, but you weren't at the party. You were so angry you were going to slug Douglas Wilmington in the middle of a very important cocktail party attended by some of the most influential people in San Francisco. If I hadn't stopped you, we'd be reading about you in the morning paper."

Hillary dropped her gaze, acknowledging the truth of his words. "If you want me to say thank you, consider it done."

Alex sighed and sat back in his seat, staring at the back of a United Airlines jet as it sped down the runway, hurtling into the sky with a roar that echoed through the silent night. "I don't want a thank-you."

"I've never seen the planes this close," Hillary said, trying to change the subject. "I usually watch takeoffs from inside the terminal."

"It's louder out here, more exciting, more vibrant. You can almost feel the power when the plane lifts to the sky." He unlocked his door and pulled the handle. "Come with me."

"Where?"

"Outside, against the fence."

Hillary sent him a doubtful look but decided that standing outside the runway in her cocktail dress was better than sitting in the car ducking his questions.

Alex met her by the fence, and she shivered at the cool night air. He immediately took off his coat and draped it around her shoulders.

"Better?"

"Yes, thanks."

Alex put his hands on the fence, linking his fingers around the wire as the next plane pulled into position. "I love coming here. There's something about flying off into the wild blue yonder that's very appealing to me."

"Run away from all your problems?"

"Something like that."

Hillary nodded, understanding the restless feeling very well. She had never thought that her desire to be a traveling journalist was tied up in wanting to run away, but maybe she was kidding herself. It was easier to stay on the go than to sit back and think about where she'd been, to remember people like Douglas Wilmington.

She had thought that part of her life was over. She had locked the experience deep inside her and had thrown away the key, never to be retrieved. But maybe that was wrong. Maybe she did need to talk to someone, get that particular weight off her shoulders. That was the only reason she was going to tell him. It had absolutely nothing to do with Alex himself or the way he made her feel. In fact, maybe talking about another man would help reinforce her decision that Alex was not for her, just as Douglas was not for her.

"We weren't lovers, but we came close," she said abruptly.

Alex turned his head, studying her profile, and then looked back at the runway. He waited for her to continue, not pressuring her in any way.

"It was a long time ago. I don't know why I reacted so strongly tonight. I guess it was the surprise that did it."

She paused as the jet in front of them began to roar. It seemed to move down the runway in slow motion, although she knew it had to be hitting speeds over a hundred miles an hour. The wheels lifted and the plane tilted, for a moment caught between earth and sky. It would either go up or come down, hard. She caught her breath, lifting the plane with her mind. And then it was up and airborne, flying off for destinations unknown.

"It's incredible that man can move so quickly from one place to another and yet I never seem to get very far," she murmured.

"Depends on what you consider far."

Hillary smiled at him. "Well, I'm not Woman of the Year. I'm not rich. I don't live in a big fancy house."

"And you don't want any of that anyway."

She tilted her head to one side. "Maybe not. I've never really wanted to be rich or even famous, just to make a difference in someone's life. My father never needed me, and my mother's sole purpose was to make my father happy. When he died, she put all her energy into turning Donna and me into the perfect wife candidates. Donna made it. I didn't pass."

"Was Wilmington your mother's choice?"

"She liked him. He had the right social connections, and he always held the door open for me." She laughed softly. "I used to hate that. It smacked of patronage. But Douglas was smart. He knew how to play the game. We were engaged before I found out about the other girls. Of course, he said they weren't important, and since I wasn't giving him what he wanted—he had to satisfy himself elsewhere. The worst thing was, everyone knew but me. I hated their pitying smiles, the knowing look in their eyes when I would go to a party. Thank God, that's all in the past."

She looked at him and shrugged her shoulders. "That's it, the whole torrid tale of adolescent love gone bad. It was years ago. I don't know why I made such a big deal out of seeing him tonight. And I do appreciate your stopping me from hitting him, although it would have given me enormous pleasure."

Alex laughed and put his arms around her waist, pulling her head just under the tuck of his chin. "Maybe I should go back and punch him for you."

"I don't think that's suitable Man of the Year behavior."

His hands moved up from her waist to her shoulders, and he rubbed the knots of tension with warm, soothing fingers. "Feel better now?"

She pulled her head off his comfortable shoulder and smiled. "Surprisingly, yes. But I don't know what it is about you that makes me want to talk. I'm usually pretty private."

"I don't know, either, but I like it."

Alex's voice was deep, tantalizingly sexy, matching the caressing movements of his fingers. In another minute she would put her arms around his neck and pull his face down to meet hers. And that would be a mistake. Hillary swallowed hard, wishing she could talk without sounding breathless. "Maybe you should take me home now. I'm tired."

"Not yet," he protested, pushing her head back against his shoulder. "This is nice. We're together, alone, and we're not arguing. It's a good place for us to start over."

Hillary thought about his words and then pulled away, even though it took all of her strength to do so. She couldn't let herself get too comfortable. And as for starting over, that was going to be a problem, too.

"Where are you going?" he asked.

"Back to the car."

"What are you afraid of?"

His question stopped her in midstride and she turned around to look at him. "I'm afraid that if we don't get back to business, we'll forget what we're supposed to be doing."

He grinned at her serious tone. "What we're supposed to be doing is getting to know each other, right?"

"But all you're doing is asking me questions."

"I have another idea, then."

"What?"

Her question went unanswered as he walked over to the car and reached inside the window to turn the key. Country music poured out of the car speaker, someone singing a song about making love in a haystack.

Hillary put her hands on her hips and stared at him in amazement. "What are you up to now?"

"You want to know something about me, right? Well, I like country music, and I like to dance." He extended his hand to her. "May I?"

"May you what?"

"Have this dance."

"Here? There are cars going by."

"One in the last half hour."

"But the planes—"

"Will love the show. You'll give the passengers something to look at while they're waiting to take off."

Alex didn't wait for her to reply. He simply grabbed her hand and pulled her over to him.

She moved like a stiff, wooden doll. "I don't dance," she said through gritted teeth.

"Why not?"

"Because I'm not good at it, another one of those feminine failings of mine. I like to lead instead of follow."

"Then lead," he encouraged. "Take me wherever you want to go. Do with me what you will. I don't care if you want to fly to the moon. Just take me with you."

Hillary stared at him wide-eyed, captivated by the magic in his voice. And her feet were moving to the tempo, in perfect accord with his body. She wasn't leading, but neither was he. They were moving in unison, their bodies in tune, even if their minds refused to agree.

"You're a romantic, Alex Donovan," she said softly, giving in to the inevitable good feelings. "And a little bit crazy. Just promise me one thing...."

"What's that?"

"If this is a dream, you won't wake me up."

Four days later the dream was gone and reality had definitely returned. After touring an art museum on Sunday, Alex had disappeared for the evening, claiming a personal appointment, and Hillary had been too exhausted by the weekend to protest. By Monday, she was eager to see him again, and disappointed to find he'd gone out of town until Wednesday. She spent the time well, researching past articles on him and studying the ups and downs of the toy business, but nothing seemed real or important without Alex to argue about it.

By the time Thursday arrived, she was edgy and nervous. She met Alex for the appointed company tour at ten o'clock in the morning and managed to maintain a cool smile as he introduced her to other employees. The efficient businessman in the conservative navy blue suit seemed a far cry from the country romantic she had danced with on the highway. Maybe it had all been a dream.

Alex also seemed a bit stiff and unyielding, not quite meeting her eye when she asked a question and always moving out of touching distance whenever she inadvertently brushed against him. Maybe he was having regrets, afraid he had let down his guard in front of a journalist shark.

She knew she could probably crucify him with tales of the airport watcher and the hopeless romantic, but didn't he know that she wouldn't do that? That she couldn't possibly destroy a moment that had been so special to them both?

Of course, he didn't know that, because he didn't trust her. For some reason that thought made her extremely depressed.

"This is the think tank," Alex said, leading her into a large sunny room on the first floor.

She looked around in surprise. Although she'd already seen dozens of toys in progress, this room was a little like stepping through the looking glass. There were balls and basketball hoops at varying levels, toy trains and rocket ships, dolls and barking dogs. A miniature island with pirate ships and skeletons was set up in one corner of the room. A telescope on a pedestal was pointed through a skylight in the roof that opened and closed with the push of a button, and a replica of the deep blue sea was set up in an enormous aquarium. Everywhere she looked, she saw bursts of fantasy and color.

"This is my latest creation, a new board game for teenagers, the kind of kids who profess they're too old for toys." Alex pointed to the table next to them.

"But you're never too old for toys, right?"

"Right. This game utilizes the computer and the traditional game board. It's also a combination murder mystery and algebra equation. They can have fun and learn something at the same time. Kids need to be challenged. Otherwise they get bored and get into real trouble."

Hillary ran her finger around the edge of the three-dimensional game board. It was colorful and inviting with a sophisticated hookup to a personal computer. "I'd love to try it when we have more time."

"Of course. So what do you think?" Alex asked, stopping in the middle of the room to study her expression.

"Wow."

For the first time that day, the shell cracked, and he smiled with genuine pleasure. "You like it?"

"Are you kidding? It's incredible. What a wonderful place to play. I feel like a five-year-old. Your staff must love coming to work here. Or should I even call it work?"

His smile faded. "Yes, you should. We work very hard at creating toys that capture the imagination of a rather cynical, jaded generation. Everything in here has been developed from a simple idea on a piece of paper through hands-on experiments with different materials and lots of different ideas. Regardless of what you think, creating toys is not child's play." He paused, shaking his head in frustation. "You don't understand this, do you? You just don't get it. I can't imagine why Roger Thornton would assign someone like you to do a story on me."

Hillary looked at him in astonishment. "Would you slow down? All I said was that this was a wonderful place to play."

"But you said it in a derogatory way, as if it merely reinforced your opinions about my business. Toy Magic is a serious operation, and it's about time you realized that."

"You're twisting my words."

He crossed his arms in front of his chest, his face set in a guarded expression. "Fine. Let's continue the tour."

"No. I want to get something straight with you. I am not here to do a hatchet job on your company." Hillary's voice softened. "I know it means a lot to you. That's why you're being so sensitive about it. If I tell you I don't like the paint on the wall, it's like saying I think your child is an ugly redhead."

Her comment brought a reluctant smile to his lips. "I'm not that bad."

"Yes, you are. You're very protective about the things you care about. I saw that when we were at the gym. You pointed everything out to me in the best possible light, afraid I would try to find something negative about the place. Now you're doing the same thing here." She paused, catching his eye. "You even wanted to punch out Douglas Wilmington on my behalf, and we've only known each other a few days."

"Then you do understand," he said quietly, drawing out a long look between them that literally sizzled with unspoken sentences. "I'm glad."

Hillary licked her lips in a nervous gesture, unsettled once again by the electricity that always seemed to flow between them. She was constantly getting little shocks, and she couldn't seem to stop them. "Is there anything else you have to show me?"

Alex nodded slowly. "Follow me."

He led her out of the think tank and down the hall toward a closed door. Turning the knob, he opened it and stepped back so she could enter. It was a conference room with a long oblong table, a video screen at one end and two narrow windows that allowed the sunlight to drift into the room in thin slits of light. It was simple in decor and completely unlike any of the other rooms she had seen at Toy Magic. Hillary gave Alex a quizzical smile that quickly faded when she saw him turn the dead bolt on the door.

"Alex?" She took a step back at the look in his eyes. Her hips came up against the end of the conference table, and she couldn't go any farther. Alex smiled at her movement and walked forward until he was standing mere inches from her body. With the differences in height, she was facing the tight knot in his tie, but if she raised her eyes slightly, she could see the rapid pulse beating in his neck.

His arms slid around her waist, pulling her up against his body. Finally she raised her eyes, wondering if she would see him smiling or serious. She was beginning to realize how unpredictable his moods were, always keeping her off balance. He was smiling now, but there was some other spark glowing in his eyes. Desire. She had seen it before and tried to forget about it. Now she knew that was going to be impossible.

"What...what are you doing?" she asked.

"Giving in to an impulse."

She swallowed hard. "I don't think this is a good idea."

"Don't think. Just feel." He lowered his head, brushing the corner of her mouth with his lips. "I'm tired of answering questions."

"But I still have some more to ask," she said desperately. She placed her hands against his chest, thinking she would push him away, but the movement only brought her closer into the circle of his arms.

"Let's see what else your mouth is good for," he murmured, slowly drawing her lips into a long, hungry kiss.

Her eyes closed in response. She couldn't think of a thing to say. The sensation of his mouth on hers was simply too good. She parted her lips, tasting the edge of his tongue, allowing him complete access to her mouth with no restraints, no pretenses.

He turned his head with a groan, capturing her mouth more deeply, pulling her body against his until she could feel every inch of his body. There was power in his embrace, and when his hands ran up and down her bare arms, she could feel the calluses on his palms, emphasizing the differences between them. Man and woman, gentle and tough, and yet they each had both qualities.

There was no distinction as their mouths mingled and lingered, moved hungrily and then with tenderness. She almost felt as if they were one person. Kissing him wasn't enough. She wanted to get closer, much closer.

She didn't know which one of them pulled away first or if the simple need for air was what broke them apart, but when it happened, Hillary could do little more than stand there, staring at him, her breath coming in ragged gasps that matched the rhythm of his chest. His tie was half-open, the top two buttons of his shirt undone where her hands had traveled unaided by her consciousness. A rush of heat flooded her face, and she put her hands to her cheeks in embarrassment.

"I—I"

"Don't say anything." Alex held up a hand. He took in a deep breath and let it out, revealing his own amazement at what had just passed between them. "I missed you."

"It was only a couple of days."

"Too long." Alex bent over and picked up her gold-plated barrette off the floor. "I guess I got a little carried away."

"We both did, and this has to stop."

Alex sat down on the edge of the conference table. "I hope you don't want me to apologize."

Hillary cleared her throat and shifted from one foot to the other, feeling vulnerable in the wake of such a heart-stopping embrace. Of course she didn't want him to apologize, unless it was to say he was sorry for stopping and not making love to her right then and there on the conference room table.

"Hillary? You can talk now. I haven't seen you this quiet since I met you." He grinned. "I guess I've found a way to shut you up."

"Are we done here?"

"Is that all you have to say?"

"No. I have to be objective to write this piece about you. I can't do that if I end up—you know—kissing you."

"At least you have firsthand knowledge of one of my talents."

Hillary walked over to the door and turned the bolt back. "I'm leaving. I am not going to play this game."

Alex followed her to the door. "This isn't a game. This is the only room in the building that is strictly business. Maybe that's why I brought you here. I wanted you to know the difference."

She stared at him for a long moment, wondering if she was reading too much or too little into his statement. "I don't know what you're talking about."

"Yes, you do. You're just afraid to admit it."

"I need to get back to work."

"One question. Where did you learn to kiss like that?"

She shook her head, helplessly acknowledging that no matter how much she tried to keep her cool, this man was determined to unsettle her. "Why don't I ask you a question instead?" She reached over and picked up his hand, turning it palm-side up. "Where did you get these calluses?"

There was no laughter left in his expression, no answering witty reply or sharp comment, just a shadow of pain. "Playing tennis at the country club."

"Right. I should have guessed."

"It's a long story." He pulled his hand away from hers. "I have time."

"But I don't. I have an appointment."

"What a coincidence."

They both reached for the door at the same time, his hand coming down on top of hers. Alex looked down into her eyes and started to laugh. "You're a magnet, Hillary."

"Unfortunately, I keep attracting trouble."

She dropped her hand and he opened the door, ushering her into the corridor. They walked quietly back toward his office where Hillary had left her coat.

"You've been gone a long time," Rosemary said sharply.

Hillary put a self-conscious hand to her hair, realizing that her barrette was still in her hand and not on her head.

"It's a big company," Alex interjected, picking up a stack of pink slips on her desk. "You've been busy this morning."

"Very. Don't forget you have a dentist's appointment in fifteen minutes."

Alex frowned. "It can't be six months yet."

"Eight months. You cancelled the last two appointments."

"Maybe I should cancel this one, too. I have a ton of work to catch up on."

"Over my dead body."

Hillary watched their confrontation with an amused smile. "Are you afraid of the dentist, Alex?"

"No, of course not. I'm just busy."

Hillary laughed, and even Rosemary allowed herself a small smile. Alex scowled at them both. "Okay, I'll go. I'll go. I suppose you want to watch?"

"No, I think I can pass on the trip to the dentist. I hate to see a grown man cry. Besides, I want to start putting some of my notes down on paper. When will I see you again? Tonight?"

Alex paused and then shook his head. "No, not tonight."

"What about tomorrow?"

"Dinner meeting with some potential investors."

Hillary started to tap one foot against the hardwood floor. "Are you stalling me?"

Alex looked at Rosemary and held out his hands. "Would you tell her my schedule, please."

"Tell her yourself."

Hillary laughed. "Go to the dentist, Alex. I'll pin you down later."

Alex picked up his keys and headed out the door. Hillary walked over to the coatrack where she had left her coat and paused. "Would you mind if I asked you a few questions, Rosemary? For the article?"

Rosemary continued typing on her computer keyboard for a moment and then stopped. "I suppose it's all right."

Hillary walked over to the front of the desk and took a seat in a stiff, uncomfortable chair that was obviously not meant to encourage visitors. "How long have you been working for Alex?"

"Five years."

"What kind of an employer is he?"

"Fair, honest and hardworking. He treats me with respect. I have no complaints." Her tone offered no shades of gray.

Hillary smiled, trying to ease the tension on the older woman's face. "I guess I don't really have to ask you anything, because it's clear from your tone that you're very loyal, and Alex must have done something right to inspire that loyalty. I just wish I could get a clearer picture of who he is away from all this. I'm sure running a multimillion-dollar company must force him to play out certain roles, act the dignified boss on occasion."

Rosemary's face lightened at the word "dignified." In fact, she came very close to smiling. Maybe she knew about Alex's tendency to dance on the highway.

"He can be a devil, but he's got a heart like an angel. Just ask anyone."

"I'm asking you. Why do you think Alex is the right choice to be Man of the Year?"

Rosemary thought about the question. "He's a successful businessman. He's also a good person, very generous to those less fortunate. I think he's a role model for young people. In fact, we have dozens of kids in here all the time.

Sometimes I think I'm working in a junior high school.'' She squared her shoulders as if she had suddenly realized she was going off track. "At any rate, I think he's a good choice for your magazine.''

"Okay, thanks.'' Hillary got to her feet, knowing that Rosemary was not going to give her any real information, at least not willingly. She stopped to pick up a photo sitting on the desk. It was a holiday picture of Rosemary and a gray-haired gentleman wearing flower leis and standing in front of a beach cabana. "Hawaii?'' she asked.

Rosemary nodded. "Alex sent my husband and me to Hawaii for our thirtieth wedding anniversary. We had a wonderful time.''

"For thirty years you deserved to have a wonderful time.''

"It's not hard to stay married that long when you pick the right man,'' Rosemary replied, giving her another sharp look. "I keep telling Alex he should settle down.''

"I'm sure if he did he would break about a million hearts.''

"But not his own.''

Hillary met her gaze head-on, seeing the speculation in Rosemary's eyes but unwilling to acknowledge even a tiny hint of it. "Thanks for letting me take up your time.''

"I'm happy to help.''

Just as long as I don't do anything to hurt your baby cub, Hillary thought as she picked up her coat and walked out of the office. Rosemary was simply more evidence of Alex's generosity. Was he really a good person or did he use his money to buy loyalty? She had yet to meet anyone who hadn't benefited by Alex's monetary goodwill. She was going to have to dig a little deeper.

Chapter Seven

The next day Hillary leaned back in her desk chair and played with the phone cord as she waited for her call to Southern California to go through. She looked up as Roger Thornton's secretary, Marie, stopped beside her desk.

"Roger wants to see you when you're free," Marie said.

"Give me ten minutes. I've been trying to get this woman all morning."

"Okay, but he's leaving for lunch at eleven-thirty today."

Hillary consulted her watch and then nodded. "I'll make it." She straightened up in her seat as a voice came over the line.

"Newsroom, this is Joan."

"Hi, Joani, Hillary here."

"Hillary. It's good to hear your voice. I was afraid you were languishing in some Caribbean jail after your last escapade."

"Please, don't remind me. Listen, I'd love to chat, but—"

"But you need a favor. What's up?"

"I'm doing a cover story on Alexander Donovan. He's going to be our Man of the Year."

"No kidding. He's not your usual style."

Hillary smiled to herself. "You can say that again. At any rate, he was born in Los Angeles and orphaned there when his parents were killed in an auto accident. The aunt he lived with after that point also died a few years later. I'm faxing you a sheet with all the particulars. Can you run a check for me? Maybe talk to J.T., see if he can put his experienced P.I. nose on this one?"

Joan hesitated. "That's a tall order, Hillary. I'm tied up on an urban housing development story right now. What are you hoping to find?"

Hillary paused for a long moment, picking up the newspaper clipping of Alex. She almost felt guilty for what she was thinking, but she couldn't help but believe that something was wrong with the picture. Alex was too wary to be completely innocent. There had to be something that he was hiding. She was almost afraid to find out what it was. If only he would confide in her, trust her. But then, why should he? He knew exactly what she would do with the information, and so did she. Unless there were extenuating circumstances. . . .

"Hillary, are you still there?"

"Sorry, I was just thinking." She took a deep breath. "What I'm looking for is a lie, a hole that he forgot to plug up, even the smallest detail like a birthdate that's the wrong year."

"I'll see what I can do," Joan replied.

"Thanks, I owe you one." Hillary hung up the phone and went to find her boss.

* * *

Roger Thornton was sitting behind his large, imposing desk, jotting notes on a yellow pad of paper while classical music played softly in the background. The lilting strains of Bach were in direct contrast to the burly individual chewing gum and swearing under his breath as he reviewed copy for another article.

"Roger?" Hillary took his grunt to mean come in and sit down, so she pulled out the chair in front of his desk and resigned herself to waiting until he was ready to speak.

"How's the story coming?" Roger asked, taking a break from his notes to look at her.

"Fine." She hoped he would leave it at that, but of course he didn't.

"Anything to report?"

"Not yet, but it's only been a week."

"Is Donovan cooperating?"

"Barely. I get the surface chitchat, the smooth answers, but nothing earth-shattering. He almost seems to be as perfect as his press release."

Roger rolled his eyes in response. "I hope you can get me more than that."

"I'm trying. I need more time."

"As long as you remember that this story is very important to the magazine, and to your career." He paused for a long moment and then said, "Howard Crawley just won an award for his profile on Senator Houston. He's itching for a D.C. assignment when Fleming retires."

Hillary's temper flared. "But I have more seniority. I've been here longer, and I've given more to this magazine than Crawley."

"You also cost us big bucks and a near diplomatic scandal." Roger waved his hand at her in frustration. "I'm behind you, Hillary, but I need some ammunition to use on our publisher. I'm hoping you can give it to me with Alexander Donovan.''

"Maybe you should have given me more to work with. He's a toymaker. I can't make him into an international spy.''

"Just find something on him. Something we can sink our teeth into. Nobody is perfect. Maybe you can get him to let down his guard.''

"How do you suggest I do that? He knows I'm a reporter. Our roles are clearly defined.''

"Then blur the lines. Come on, Hillary, use your imagination.''

Blur the lines? Hillary sighed. She'd already done that by kissing the man until she was breathless, but she certainly wasn't going to tell Roger Thornton that.

"Where are you two going next?'' Roger asked.

"Probably another party. That seems to be his specialty.''

"Keep me posted.''

"I will.'' Hillary got to her feet and walked out of the office as Roger picked up the phone and punched out a series of numbers.

"What do you think? Do you want to go another mile?'' Alex slowed his run down to a jog as he looked over at Hillary, who was trying to catch her breath. His eyes lit up with amusement. "You're out of shape for a tough reporter.''

Yes, she was, Hillary silently admitted, but then she wasn't used to running four miles through Golden Gate Park at seven o'clock on a Saturday morning.

"I'm better after my morning coffee,'' she gasped, as she rubbed a hand over the stitch in her side. "Do you do this every day?''

"At least four times a week," Alex said, slowing his pace to hers.

Hillary looked at him out of the corner of her eye. If there was one thing he was telling the truth about, it was probably his love for running. You didn't get strong, lean legs like his by sitting behind a desk all day. He probably used the weights at the gym, as well, because the running shirt he had chosen revealed well-defined muscles in the arms and across the chest.

Suddenly it was a little harder to catch her breath. Checking out Alex's body had done nothing to lower her blood pressure. In running shorts and a tank top, he looked like someone she wanted to work up a sweat with, but not necessarily on the jogging trails.

"You really like exercise, don't you?"

"Running is a natural high," Alex said. "With the blood pumping, my creativity gets a jump start. By the time I get to the office, I've got ideas singing through my brain."

Hillary looked at his cheerful face and shook her head in dismay. "My God. You're a morning person, aren't you? One of those people who wakes up, jumps out of bed and sings, 'Oh, What a Beautiful Day.'"

Alex laughed, the corners of his mouth turning up in a teasing smile. "Don't tell me you're a grump?"

"No, I'm not, but my body needs a little time to kick into gear." She moved over to one side of the path as a group of joggers passed them going the opposite direction. She had to admit that running through the park on a beautiful sunny morning wasn't a bad way to start the day, especially with Alex at her side. In fact, she had actually felt a sudden zip of excitement when he had showed up on her doorstep just after six-thirty that morning, which was a small miracle, considering her sleepy state.

"Are you tired?" Alex asked.

"A little. I'm sure my muscles will be complaining tomorrow."

"Not after the first mile. Once you get warmed up—"

"Hold on. Tomorrow is Sunday, the day of rest."

"You're supposed to be my shadow, Hillary."

"Then why is it I only get to shadow you at certain times of the day?"

"I have to have some privacy."

"Why?" Hillary stopped abruptly, and Alex ran into her, grabbing her around the waist so they wouldn't topple over.

"You never stop running like that, Hillary. You've got to slow down and let your heart get back to normal."

Hillary leaned over and rested her hands on her knees, feeling a little light-headed.

Alex took her arm and pulled her up straight. "Come on, keep walking, and you'll feel better."

He moved them both over to the side of the path and her dizziness passed.

"Better now?"

"Yes. Can I stop now without running the risk of a heart attack?"

He nodded. "I think so."

"Good, because I have a question, and I want an answer, right here, right now, no excuses. Are you ready?"

He hesitated. "I feel like I should have my hand on a sixshooter, in case you try to put a bullet through my heart."

Hillary stared at him, wondering if that wasn't exactly what she was trying to do. "I'm not trying to hurt you."

"I know. I was being overly dramatic. Go ahead. Ask me your earth-shattering question. Wait. Let me guess. You want to know if the sheets on my bed are really purple satin. Right?"

Hilary made a face. "I don't care about your bed. And I'm not going to let you joke your way out of this. I have a question, and I'd like an answer." She started walking again, feeling stronger and more sure of herself while they were walking. The constant movement seemed to lessen the intensity between them.

"Okay, this is it." She took a deep breath. "If you and I were involved in a personal way..." Her words drifted off at the sudden sparkle in his eyes, and she raised a hand in warning. "This is purely theoretical."

"Too bad. Go on."

"If we were together in a relationship, a serious relationship, would you tell me about yourself? Would you trust me with information that you wouldn't necessarily give a reporter?"

Alex stopped walking, and she had no choice but to do the same. His smile had faded and his lips were drawn up in a tight, harsh line. "If that was your plan, you've blown it by telling me up-front."

"It wasn't my plan. But I wonder if it should have been. Are there any women in your life, besides the ones I've seen hanging around you at the parties? Is there someone special? Someone that you share your secrets with?"

"So you want to know the name of my lover, or lovers, as the case may be?"

"Not a name. I just want to know if you trust anybody or if its just me that seems to come up against a wall of concrete."

Alex started to speak, but when two women came up the path behind him, he took her arm in a strong, almost painful grip and led her off the main path. He didn't stop until they were dark in the shadow of a thicket of trees. It was difficult to see the sun from here, even the singing of the birds was blocked out. It was quiet, dark, and distinctly unsettling. A path of goose bumps ran down her bare arms as a breeze chilled the sweat on her skin.

Alex propped one leg on the edge of a tree stump and stared at a squirrel running through the leaves. "There's never been anyone special," he said. "At least not in the way you mean. I like women, and we enjoy each other's company, but as for sharing pillow talk, no. There was a woman back a few years, before I had any money, who was interesting. But she found a better prospect, and she moved on. Looking back, it was probably for the best. She hated airplanes."

Hillary ignored the smile on his lips, realizing it was bitter in tone and barely covering a long-buried pain of rejection. "That must have hurt you."

"The pain was fairly sharp at the time, but I survived. It's not hard to survive, you know. It's much harder to die."

She looked at him in surprise, waiting for him to go on, but he fell silent, obviously regretting his choice of words. "Are you saying that you wanted to die? Over this woman?"

"No, not over her." He shook his head. "I don't know what I'm saying. Forget it." He started to walk away, but Hillary grabbed his arm.

"Don't go, Alex. Don't say something and then leave me hanging. It's not fair."

He shook her hand off his arm. "Look, I was just being dramatic. I was never suicidal, so you can forget that angle for your story."

Her story. The words brought her goal sharply back into focus, but the truth was that she wanted to know for herself, for her relationship with Alex, not for the magazine. But he would never believe that. And she couldn't blame him.

"I understand," she said finally.

"No, you don't. How could you? You grew up in a fairy tale with a father you worshipped and a mother who made Donna Reed look like a fraud. You had a sister to share secrets with, probably a white canopy bed to sleep in." He placed his hands on his waist in a belligerent manner, daring her to defy his image of her. "Your biggest problem was probably trying to get your mother to let you wear a miniskirt to school."

Hillary immediately shook her head. "Never. Not true. I wouldn't have been caught dead with a silly froth of material over my bed. And I never even wanted to wear a dress, much less a mini. I was a tomboy, Alex." She pulled at her ponytail for emphasis. "I cut off all my hair when I was eleven, so I could play on the boy's Little League team. Yes, my mother did bake cookies when we came home from school, and yes she did try to make me into the little princess, but it didn't work. I was a square peg she was trying to shove into a round hole."

The tension on Alex's face lessened as she spoke. "Did you really cut off your hair?"

"Yes, with garden shears. My mother was so embarrassed she wouldn't go to the PTA meetings for a month. Donna tried to disown me and even locked me in my room when she had a friend come over so I wouldn't be seen. You want to know about rejection? Believe me, I could write a book about it."

Alex gave her a reluctant smile. "What about the boys? What did they think of your new hairstyle?"

Hillary shrugged. "I have no idea. I never thought about boys much, and when I did, I didn't have a clue what to do. My sister was the sexy one, always wearing the right clothes and getting nominated for things like prom queen. I was skinny and I wore braces for years, and I preferred playing football to watching it. I never had a date. Didn't even go to the senior prom.''

"Neither did I," Alex said. With a sudden movement, he bridged the distance between them, placing both hands on her waist and pulling her up against his body. "Those boys didn't know what they were missing."

"They were missing a feminine princess, that's what they were missing," she said, trying not to get sucked in by the look in his eyes. "Nobody wanted a tomboy who didn't know how to flirt. I learned that lesson a long time ago."

"And Douglas Wilmington reinforced it," Alex replied, caressing her cheek with his hand. "But you still don't see yourself the way I see you." His hand tilted her chin upward, so she could look into his eyes.

Barely breathing, Hillary murmured, "And how do you see me?"

"Wanting to be tough, but having the softest skin of anyone I've ever met."

"That's because your hands are so hard—from playing tennis, right?"

"I have done some physical work in my life. I'm not ashamed of my calluses."

"Then why do you lie about them?" Hillary challenged.

"I don't know. I guess they don't quite fit my image. And some women are turned off by rough hands." He ran his hands down her bare arms. "Are you?"

"No," she whispered.

"Good, because every time I kiss you, I want to do it again and again and again." His voice dropped to a husky murmur as his lips touched her mouth.

Hillary's hands slid up under his loose T-shirt, caressing the strong planes of his stomach, feeling the muscles clench under her fingers as his tongue pursued the depths of her mouth. He smelled like sweat and soap and everything masculine. She closed her eyes, reveling in the sensations he was drawing out of her.

She had never felt a need for a man, a deep intense longing to be a part of someone, not until now. It was a primitive surge, a wanting with abandon and recklessness. So tempting to give in. To forget about everything but this man and this moment.

Alex's mouth left hers so suddenly she felt cold, but then his lips trailed a hot path down her face to the curve of her shoulder, promising more, much more.

"How do you feel about pine needles?" Alex asked in a rough, tender voice. "Because in another minute you're going to be flat on your back."

"Or maybe you will," she replied with a challenging smile. "I've never been easy."

"Better yet. I'd like to have you on top of me, among other things."

"Alex, we have to stop this."

He shook his head, pulling the rubber band out of her hair so the blond waves could tumble around her shoulders. "I can't stop. You're addictive. Worse than chocolate chip cookies."

"Is that your favorite food?"

"It used to be, until I tasted you."

"Alex," she complained. "That's enough. I can't keep up with you."

Alex shook a finger at her. "The problem with you is that you don't have any romance in your soul."

No, the problem was she had too much, Hillary thought. That's why she was allowing herself to fantasize about Alex, about being with him in a very personal way, pine needles and all. She had to stop losing sight of her objective. "I have to go to work," she said abruptly, withdrawing from his embrace.

Alex's arms dropped to his side, and the grimness returned to his face. "More questions?"

"You still haven't answered the last one." She paused, gathering her thoughts together. "I feel like I'm caught in the middle, being squeezed from both sides. I have a job to do, a story I want to write, but then we start talking and everything else seems to fade away. I can't keep my mind on business."

"And that's so terrible?"

"Yes, it is. I have goals that I've set, things I want to accomplish. Getting personally involved with you is not one of them."

"So add another goal."

Hillary shook her head. "There's no point. I can't be the woman you want me to be."

"How do you know what I want?" Alex asked in amazement. "You think that every man wants a Barbie doll, but that isn't so."

Hillary planted her hands on her hips. "You know, you're very good at analyzing me, but when it comes to you, everything is off limits. I know nothing about your personal life except that you wake up happy and like to jog at an ungodly hour. You say I don't know what you want in a woman. Then tell me, what do you want? Someone to stay home and cook for you and be a homemaker and have 2.7 children and a dog? That's what you said in your last interview."

Alex opened his mouth and then shut it, obviously caught up in his own statements. "That was an interview for a homemaker magazine. It was geared toward an audience of women who stay at home and care for their families."

"Then you're saying that's not what you want?"

"Oh, hell, I don't know. I don't think much about marriage. I'm not sure I even believe in it, and I know I've never met anyone who made me want to believe in it." He paused for a long moment. "I'm basically a loner at heart. I depend on myself, and I take care of myself. I'm not sure I'd be very good at taking care of anyone else. I like my space."

"So do I. Which is why this flirting has to stop. There's no future for us, and no point in starting something we can't finish. I'm afraid I don't believe in affairs."

"Too bad."

His words rang with sincerity and regret, and Hillary turned away from his perceptive eyes, not wanting to reveal any of the mixed emotions running through her mind. Her thoughts and beliefs had always been cut and dried, until now, until Alex. Nothing was the same.

"Ready to finish our run?" Alex asked.

"I guess. We still need to talk, though."

"Right. I almost forgot. The story, always the story. That's the only reason you're with me, isn't it? When the article is done, you'll forget all about me."

"And you'll forget about me," she retorted. "It probably won't take more than one party of women fawning over you to do it. That's why you're out there in high society, isn't it? You're trying to prove to that woman from your past that you made it, that she should be sorry she dumped you."

"No. I don't even think about her anymore."

"You can lie to me, Alex, but don't lie to yourself."

"I'm not, but you're trying to change the subject. We're talking about you and me, no one else. I know I won't be able to forget you, because you're different."

"Exactly. I don't fit in with you and your life-style, Alex. I couldn't spend my life on a boat for one thing."

He smiled. "We'll give up the yachting parties."

"But it's everything else. I don't want to be a pretender. I want to be free to state my opinions and to live with people that respect that freedom. I can't fit into a mold of tradition. I don't even want to try. I did once, you know, with Douglas. It wasn't me then, and it isn't me now. It's nothing personal, but—"

"Oh, it's very personal, Hillary. And I think you're wrong. Dashing around the globe is not going to let you forget me or this."

He pulled her back into his arms with a purposeful gesture. Anger and passion sparked in one long searing look between them, but Hillary didn't back away. She wanted to prove that his touch meant nothing to her, and it was easy in the beginning. His mouth was hard and rough, demanding, and she had never been one to give in to pressure. But then the kiss changed. It got softer, tender, persuasive. It was good, too good, and a soft moan escaped through her parted lips when he let her go.

In the quiet park the only sound was their heavy breathing and the pounding of their hearts. Finally, Alex turned and started jogging away, leaving her to follow or to go in the other direction. It was a small decision and certainly not one to sweat over, but in a way, symbolic of everything between them. She decided to follow, moving from a slow jog to a quick run as he veered out of sight. She was suddenly panic-stricken that she would lose him, not in the trees or the park, but forever.

Chapter Eight

He lied! The accusation rang through Hillary's head like a clanging church bell at high noon. She held the telephone receiver away from her ear and stared bleakly out the window. The skyline of San Francisco met her gaze. It was a gorgeous Wednesday, the tall buildings standing out against a clear blue sky, but at the edge of the city a blanket of fog waited until nightfall, ready to cover the city. To creep in like a thief in the night, waiting until you were vulnerable and unable to run. Like Alex.

He had smiled at her like the sun, hiding a packet of lies behind those sparkling green eyes. She had let herself get taken in, even knowing that he was smooth and wily. Somewhere along the line she had started to trust him. She didn't know when. Maybe when he had taken her to the gym. Or maybe when they had watched the planes take off. She had let down her guard, and he had snuck into her heart.

The betrayal cut her deeply.

"Hillary, are you there?" Joan demanded. "Hillary?"

She stared down at the phone, wondering where the irate voice was coming from and then it came back to her. She held the receiver up to her ear. "Sorry, I got sidetracked." Hillary picked up Alex's file and flipped to his dossier, anger dousing her pain. "You said there's no record of the death of Rosie and Harold Donovan?"

"Right. Those people, whoever they were, don't exist as far as the Social Security Department is concerned. The only Harold Donovan listed died in 1926 in Omaha, Nebraska. Too early for your man. No Rosie Donovan. No record of an auto accident in Los Angeles county in the year you gave me. Are you sure you have your facts right?"

"I think so." Hillary sighed, staring down at Alex's smiling face. "Damn you," she muttered. "What are you hiding?"

"Pardon me?" Joan demanded.

"Not you, him."

"Oh, good. Listen, I have to run, but I did want to mention one last thing. The woman Alex lived with while attending Kentmoor High in Los Angeles was named Stella Banks. As far as I can tell, she wasn't a relation. There was a record of her death. Heart attack at the age of sixty-eight. After that, there's nothing until Alex resurfaced at a toy company working as a janitor. I think you know the rest."

"Yes, the rags-to-riches story. Thanks, Joani. Let me know if anything else comes up. If I have to, I'll fly down to L.A. and do my own investigating." Hillary slowly hung up the phone, her mind whirling with dozens of possibilities.

The cover was broken. Alex Donovan was not who he said he was. But who was he? That was the real question.

And why hadn't any other interviewers come up with the information? Probably because no one had cared enough to dig. The only articles he had done were celebrity interviews. Apparently the tabloids had never gotten wind of a scandal or surely they would have jumped right in. Alex had just been lucky, until now.

Getting up from her chair, she paced restlessly around her small cubicle, walking around her office chair until she started to get dizzy. She tried to remember everything he had told her about his parents and realized it amounted to nothing. Except for saying they had died, he had given her no other information. He had mentioned that life was tough, but she had attributed that to the death of his parents. Now she was beginning to wonder if she had overlooked some good clues.

And his father. He had never said anything about the man. Pausing in her pacing, she leafed through the pages of the last interview he had done. Skimming the lines with one finger, she stopped at the mention of Harold Donovan, dentist.

Dentist? She looked at the stark black letters until her eyes hurt. It didn't make sense. Alex hated the dentist. Maybe he hated his father, too. The words came unbidden into her mind, and once there she couldn't dismiss the thought that something terrible must have happened to Alex way back when, something he didn't want anyone else to know. But what?

She closed the pages of the magazine. She had to talk to Alex. There was no point in flying down to Los Angeles until he had a chance to answer her questions. There was always a possibility he would tell her the truth, come clean. Or maybe she should try Micky.

A smile crossed her face. Yes, Micky Gallant might be a better start. He said he and Alex had been friends for a long time. She would just have to be smart about what questions she asked. He wasn't going to tell her anything willingly. She needed an angle.

Alex peered through the blinds of Micky's office and groaned as a snappy red Mazda came into sight. Hillary. Just his luck. Four days had passed since they had gone jogging. He had thought it would be enough to get her out of his system, but one look, and he was hot and sweaty. He let the blinds fall back into place as the door opened behind him.

Micky raised one eyebrow at his startled look and then dropped a pile of towels on the top of his desk. "You look like you just saw the tax collector."

"I thought you were Hillary. She just pulled up out front."

Micky grinned. "No kidding. I was hoping she'd come back, but sometime when you weren't around." He snapped a towel at Alex's midsection.

Alex stepped back with a frown. "Maybe it's better that I'm here. She won't be able to do much with me standing right in front of her."

"And neither will I," Micky complained. "If you aren't interested, why don't you get lost and let me have a shot?"

Alex gave him an irritated look. "She's not here to check you out. She's snooping, looking for some dirt on me."

"And maybe your ego is working overtime. Her visit here might be strictly personal."

"No way. The woman is a sharp journalist, and I've been stalling her. She's smart enough to know that she should talk to you." He jerked around and flipped up the blind again, just in time to see Hillary stepping out of her car with a gym bag. His eyes narrowed suspiciously, and he turned around, giving Micky a quizzical look. "What's going on?"

Micky cleared his throat. "Did I mention that I'm starting a woman's self-defense class this afternoon?"

"No, you didn't."

"Really? I thought I had."

"And you invited Hillary?"

"Actually, it was her idea. Seems she and a couple of her friends have been wanting to learn some basic defense techniques. She was impressed with the setup here and asked if I'd consider taking on a few women."

Alex made a face. "And you believed her?"

Micky shrugged. "Frankly, Donovan, it's money in my pocket. Why should I complain?"

Alex started to say something but was interrupted by a knock at the door.

"Come in," Micky called out.

Hillary walked in with a jaunty smile, her blond hair pulled back into a ponytail on top of her head. She was dressed in sweats and a T-shirt, certainly nothing provocative, but Alex still felt a jangle at the end of every nerve. Unwilling to admit that she was getting to him, he growled at her, "What are you doing here?"

Hillary shrugged. "Taking a few lessons from Micky. Do you have a problem with that?"

"As a matter of fact—"

"Hold on, kids," Micky interrupted. "If you want to go a couple of rounds, I'll get you both some gloves and we'll do it in the ring, not my office."

"I'm sorry." Hillary sent Alex a dark look. "But I'm not here to argue, just to learn a few tips."

"About me," Alex muttered.

"Are your friends here yet?" Micky asked, ignoring Alex completely as he walked over to take Hillary's arm.

"Let me show you around. This is a good time of the day because the boys are in school. That's one of my requirements, that they attend at least a few classes a week. Anyway, we'll have some privacy. If this works, I may even extend a few classes to the high school girls. I've been thinking about it for a while but wasn't sure if the two would mix. The boys get pretty territorial about this place."

"I've noticed," Hillary replied, flinging Alex an amused smile as she walked into the main part of the gym with Micky at her side.

"Where are your friends?" Alex asked, coming up on Hillary's other side.

"They'll be here." She turned around as the main door opened. "In fact, they're here right now." She waved to the two women entering the gym. Like Hillary, they were dressed for a workout, but their expressions were a little more skeptical than excited.

"They look thrilled," Alex commented.

"They were a little concerned about the neighborhood," Hillary conceded. "But we're all reporters, and we have to be comfortable walking around in areas like this."

Alex gave her a disbelieving look but remained quiet while Hillary introduced Karen and Lucy to Micky.

"Are you staying or leaving?" Hillary asked Alex as the other women put their bags down on the bench. "Didn't you say you had a lunch meeting today, which is why we couldn't possibly get together?"

"Right."

"We wouldn't want you to be late."

Alex shook his head. "I don't know what you're up to here, but I don't think I like it. You're supposed to be interviewing me."

"Which I would be doing if you stopped canceling our appointments. As it is, I'm just taking a self-defense class on my lunch hour. I don't have anything to hide," she added more strongly, wishing he would just open up and confide in her, but he remained silent. The knife of betrayal cut through her again.

"Implying that I do?" Alex countered.

"If the shoe fits..."

"Yo, Alex, you want to help?" Micky called.

Alex shook his head, giving Hillary another imperceptible look. "No, I have a lunch meeting."

Micky nodded and began instructing the other women in some basic warm-up stretches while Hillary and Alex stared at each other uncertainly.

"We need to talk," Hillary said quietly. "Not just about the story but everything else."

A dark shadow crossed his face and then he slowly nodded. "I think so. Pretending you've gone away hasn't exactly worked."

"Not for me, either. What about tonight?"

"No, I can't."

She sighed. "Tomorrow night?"

"Friday night would be best. I have to run out to Sacramento tomorrow, and I may stay overnight. It really is business."

"Okay. Friday night, then."

"We'll go to dinner."

"Alone?"

He smiled. "Just you and me in a dark corner with a bottle of wine."

Hillary stiffened herself against the image. "Just make sure you're willing to talk. We're running out of time."

"Hillary, are you going to join us or stand there and flirt all day?" Lucy called out.

Hillary laughed. "I'm coming. Goodbye, Alex."

"Have a good workout."

Hillary tipped her head in acknowledgment and walked over to join the others, conscious of Alex's lingering gaze. Then he was gone, and she was struck by the long, cold shiver that always seemed to accompany his departure.

"Okay, ladies, first thing we're going to do is learn how to walk. You're going to go through the big city a lot differently than you take a walk through a country garden." He motioned for Hillary to come forward. "I want you to look tough and act tough. Think you can do that?"

Hillary nodded. She had been practicing those particular moves for a very long time.

By the time class ended, Hillary was sweaty and breathless from the exertion of Micky's instruction. He was a demanding instructor, and she realized halfway through the session that her ploy for finding out about Alex from Micky was going to take a tremendous amount of energy. Even her friends had lost their skepticism and gotten into the action.

"Next week, ladies?" Micky asked at the end of class.

"I'm on," said Lucy, with Karen nodding agreement.

"Sounds good to me," Hillary replied. She dawdled while the other women picked up their bags and left the gym. Then she smiled brightly at Micky, who was already walking to the other side of the gym where the weight machines were located. "It's too bad Alex decided not to stay. I think he would have been impressed at how much we learned."

Micky began to move between the machines, checking the weights. "I wondered when you were going to get around to him."

"Saw right through me, huh?"

He looked up and grinned. "But I made you sweat for it."

She nodded. "Actually, that was great, better than I expected. I really do think the class is valuable."

"So do I. Neither of us wasted our time."

"How did you meet Alex?" The question came out more abruptly than she had intended, but it didn't even faze Micky. He sat down on one of the benches and placed his legs under the weight bar, lifting it up and down as he checked the smoothness of the machine.

"I met him in high school," he said.

"What high school? Kentmoor?"

"Yes."

Hillary sighed when he refused to offer more. "Okay, you met in school. Was Alex a good student?"

"No, he dropped out when he was seventeen."

So he was as familiar with Alex's bio as she was. "That's right after his aunt died. Did you know her, too?"

"Sure. Everyone knew Stella. She was quite a character, but she had a soft spot for Alex. He wasn't a cute kid, kind of scrawny and always had a look on his face that said 'Don't mess with me.' We actually met in the middle of a fight on the playground. Somebody made fun of my tennis shoes. They were full of holes and some godawful color. I don't remember who started it, but suddenly there were about ten fifteen-year-olds slugging it out." He smiled at the memory. "Alex came out on top and so did I. Been friends ever since."

"Then you knew Alex before he was a millionaire?"

"Hell, yes. I knew him when he didn't have two pennies to rub together."

"Was he different then?" Hillary asked with interest.

"Not really. He's always been a loner. Now he seems to have a few more friends, but not too many people get close." Micky looked at her through narrowed eyes. "When Alex likes someone, he takes care of them, looks out for their interests, whatever it takes."

Hillary looked at him for a long moment, trying to read between the lines, understand the gleam in his eyes. "In other words, if Alex was covering up something, he would have a good reason, like friendship."

"I don't think I said he was covering up anything."

Hillary gave him a wry smile. "You're not going to help me, are you?"

"I just did. Think about what I said. The answer will come to you."

"I hope it comes soon. I only have two more weeks to write this story."

Micky got to his feet. "If worse comes to worst, you can always ask Alex to tell you the truth."

"Do you think he would?" Hillary challenged.

Micky tipped his head, considering her thoughtfully. "For you, I think there's a possibility. Give him a chance. Now get out of here. I've got sixteen teenagers coming in half an hour, and I don't need you distracting them."

Hillary extended her hand. "Thanks, Micky."

"For what?"

"I don't know yet, but when I figure it out, I'll let you know."

He smiled and shook her hand. "Deal."

By the time Friday night rolled around, Hillary was tense and on edge. She had spent the past two days debating whether she should confront Alex and risk the possibility of him cutting her off completely or whether she should bide her time and hope he would open up on his own.

It was going to be hard to pretend that she didn't know something was up. She had never been a good game player.

She just didn't have a poker face. As she ran a brush through her hair and flicked a nervous look at her watch, Micky's words came back into her mind. *When Alex likes someone, he takes care of them, looks out for their interests, whatever it takes*. It was such a simple statement. There had to be more to it.

Tossing the hairbrush down on the side table, she shrugged her arms into the white sweater she wore over her deep turquoise blue dress. Maybe the evening would shed some light. Alex was due to pick her up in ten minutes for a late dinner at Martinelli's Italian Café. She would eat pasta, drink some wine and hopefully mellow Alex into telling her something of value. If not, she was going to have no other choice but to confront him with his lies.

The doorbell rang and she walked over to answer it, taking one last look around her apartment to make sure everything was in order. It also gave her another chance to catch her breath. Every time she saw the man, the wind got knocked out of her.

The bell rang again, more impatiently this time, as if Alex was eager to see her. A tiny glow of excitement grew brighter at the thought, and she refused to dampen it with any gloomy thoughts.

She opened the door and smiled. "Hi."

Alex looked at her for a long time, his green eyes serious and intense, as if he were trying to figure out a very complicated puzzle. And then his gaze softened as he moved down from her eyes to her lips. It was such a sweet, longing look. She almost felt as though he had kissed her.

"Do you want to come in?" she asked belatedly, realizing that standing and staring at each other in the hall was probably not the best idea. Although if he did come inside...

Alex shook his head, reading her thoughts with a sharp, perceptive smile. "I don't think that would be a good idea. Unless you're planning to skip dinner?"

Her heart jumped at the thought. It would be foolish, irresponsible, completely crazy, so why was she even hesitating? His name came through her lips in a husky whisper, and his mouth tightened into a grim line.

"Don't say my name like that, not unless you mean business."

"I always mean business."

Alex shook his head, dropping the hand that he had instinctively reached out to her. "We better go. I'm sure you're hungry."

"Yes," she agreed, allowing his abruptness to cool the heat in her body. She picked up her purse from the table and locked the door behind her.

They walked quietly out to his car. He had brought the Mercedes again, although she knew he often drove the Jeep for pleasure. Obviously he wanted to remind her of the formality of their date. He was a businessman, and she was a reporter. That was the extent of their relationship. It had to be.

Alex opened the door for her like a perfect gentleman and she refrained from making a feminist remark, knowing that it would only be a cover for the way she was feeling, which was soft and vulnerable, not tough and independent.

Alex slid into his seat without a word and turned the key in the ignition while she fastened her seat belt.

"Ready?" he asked with a brief glance in her direction.

"Yes. Where is Martinelli's?"

"Downtown. They have wonderful food. I think you'll like it." He checked the rearview mirror and then pulled away from the curb. The evening traffic was light at this end of town, but she knew the cars would be thicker as they got into the heart of the city.

"I love pasta," Hillary said idly, "although I may need another run tomorrow."

"I'm busy tomorrow."

His harsh words brought her gaze to his face. "I wasn't asking you to go with me."

"Oh? I didn't realize you jogged on your own."

"I can do just about anything on my own."

"I forgot. You don't need anybody, right?"

"Right. Just like you, Mr. Donovan."

Alex let a few minutes of tense silence pass before letting out a weary sigh. He took a glance over his shoulder and then pulled over to the side of the street. Throwing the car into park, he let the motor run while he turned to look at her.

"Are we there?" Hillary asked.

"No. But I can't drive and argue with you at the same time."

"Are we arguing?"

"It feels like it."

Hillary crossed her arms in front of her waist and stared straight ahead. "I was making small talk. You were the one who jumped down my throat."

"I know." His quiet tone brought her head around. "I didn't want to see you tonight. It's easier when I just think about you from a distance. When we get close, I lose sight of what we're supposed to be doing." He waved a hand in the air in frustration. "What am I going to do about you? Should I ask the magazine to assign someone else to my story?"

"No." The answer flew out of her mouth sharp and anguished. "You can't do that. I've done nothing wrong."

"I'm not trying to hurt you, Hillary. I just think it might be better for both of us to call a halt. You've already said you don't want to get involved with me, but we both know there's something going on between us."

Hillary put a hand to her throat, forcing herself to swallow before answering. "We can keep things professional," she said finally. "It just takes a little more effort. And if you will give me some undivided time this weekend, we can wrap up the article by next week. Then I can get out of your life."

"What if I don't want you to?"

"Alex, you just said—"

"I know what I said." He drummed his fingers restlessly on the steering wheel.

"You can't take me off this story. It would hurt my career. If you have any feelings about me, you won't do that."

He turned to look at her, and there was something like disappointment in his eyes. "Your career means everything to you, doesn't it?"

"It means a lot. Can't you understand that? You've been driving yourself to build an empire over the last ten years. Why should it be different for me?"

He shook his head. "I guess it shouldn't." He straightened in his seat. "Let's get something to eat."

Hillary put a hand on his arm, and he quickly removed it, his breath speeding up at the touch.

"Hands off, or I'll forget our pact."

"I just wanted to say thank you."

"Don't thank me, yet. You may live to regret this decision."

He started the car and then paused as the car phone buzzed. "Do you mind? Only a few people have this number. It must be important."

Hillary shook her head. "Go ahead."

"Hello."

"Alex? Is that you, man?"

"Rocky?" Alex looked at Hillary and then tightened his hand on the phone. "What's wrong?"

"I ran away. I messed up the Jenkinses' car. They were going to kick me out, anyway."

"Oh, hell. Where are you?"

"Corner of Mission and Third. I need some bus money. Then I'll hit the road."

"Just stay put. I'll be there in ten minutes."

Alex hung up the phone and gunned the motor as he pulled away from the curb. Hillary flinched as they ran a yellow light turning red.

He flung her a quick look. "Sorry, but we have to make a stop."

"Someone's in trouble?"

"Yes, a stupid punk kid." Alex shook his head in frustration. "He doesn't know when he has it good."

Hillary didn't know what he was talking about, but she sensed that whoever had been on the other end of the phone was a good friend of Alex's. Another one. For a man who claimed he was a loner, there sure were a lot of people in his life.

Chapter Nine

Their trip across San Francisco was fast, with Alex maneuvering around double-parked cars and stodgy buses with the agility of a race car driver. Once again they bypassed the sophisticated downtown area and headed for one of the streets on the edge of the city. As they got closer to their destination, Alex slowed the car down and began to peer closely at the buildings along the sidewalk.

"Who are we looking for?" Hillary asked. "Maybe I can help."

"A twelve-year-old with big feet and a bigger mouth."

"You're not giving me much to go on."

"There he is," Alex said, cutting across the traffic to the curb. This side of the street was empty of passersby, the local print shop having closed for the day. But there was a lone figure standing in front of a telephone booth. Alex unlocked the door and stepped out. "Stay here, Hillary. Let me handle this, okay? And keep the doors locked."

"Okay." Hillary watched as Alex walked over to the boy, who was wearing a baseball cap, a ragged T-shirt and blue jeans. On his feet were a pair of oversize tennis shoes. His dirty-blond hair was on the long side with a tail down the back, and he looked as if he'd been on the street for a while. Another stray cat, she thought, tapping her fingers restlessly on her purse. Alex did seem to collect them.

Alex put a hand on the boy's arm. Whatever he was saying was making the boy very uncomfortable. He kept looking at the ground and shuffling his big feet. Once in a while he looked up and made his own argument, but it was quickly taken apart by Alex.

Confident that Alex was handling his young friend, Hillary looked idly around her. This part of the block didn't boast much more than a couple of rundown shops closed for the night and an empty parking lot. Just down the street, behind the car, there was an apartment building with bars across the lower windows. It was then that Hillary noticed two older boys hovering in one of the doorways. They were staring straight at Alex.

Hillary tensed, suddenly seeing Alex in the glare of the streetlight as they did—a prime, juicy target. His car and his suit cried money, and his gold cufflinks glittered in the darkness, a beacon calling out to the youths. It didn't take long before they moved.

Hillary's only thought was to warn Alex. She forgot about his admonition to stay in the car with the doors locked. She had never been a passive bystander, and she wouldn't be one now. Unfortunately, when she opened the car door, everyone's attention turned to her. She was standing on the sidewalk caught between Alex and the boy on one side and the two older youths on the other.

"Get in the car," Alex commanded. His voice was firm and unyielding.

Hillary hesitated, looking warily around her. "Why don't we all get in the car?"

"Why don't we?" one of the tough-looking boys said with a sneer. He was at her side before Alex could move, entwining his dirty fingers in her blond hair, yanking her head so far back it hurt. "Not bad," he said, stroking her exposed neck with the other hand.

A surge of panic ran through her body as the boy's hand tightened around her hair in a painful grip.

"Let go of her." Alex took an aggressive step toward them.

"Maybe I will and maybe I won't. She's kind of cute."

"Touch her and you're dead."

The boy laughed at Alex's threat. "Who's going to do it? You?"

Alex put a hand on Rocky's shoulder and shoved him toward the car. Rocky ran out into the street, sliding into the back seat of the car on the driver's side.

Hillary tried to see what the other teenager was doing. He was standing a few feet away, ready to pounce if necessary. Her brief self-defense lesson had not prepared her for this situation, and she tried desperately to think of a solution.

Then something cool slid against her throat. Her eyes widened at the knife glancing off her skin. Oh, Lord, she was going to die. The urge to close her eyes and hope it was a nightmare almost overcame her good sense. She had to keep her wits about her. They were on a street corner. People just didn't get killed on street corners, did they? Not that anyone seemed to be paying any attention to the scenario being played out on the curb. The people in their cars probably couldn't see what was going on, blocked by the streetlights and parked cars, and there was no one else on the sidewalk.

"Let's see your wallet, dude," the boy ordered. "Kick it over here, real slow."

Alex hesitated and then did what he said, moving very subtly toward them as he did so. Hillary saw the movement, as the boy holding her called out to his friend to check the cash. The other youth sauntered forward and flipped open the billfold, calling out to his partner that they had struck gold.

The grip on her hair lessened as the boy holding her was unable to resist taking a look. That's when Alex moved, knocking the knife out of the boy's hand before he could do more than flinch. Hillary ducked out of his grasp as Alex was attacked by the other kid from behind.

She stared at the scene in horror, wanting to do something to stop them from hurting him. Looking frantically around for a stick or something she could use in defense, she saw a large rock at the edge of the pavement, obviously part of the construction going on across the street. She picked up the rock and paused. Alex and the boys were wrestling so closely, she was afraid she would hit the wrong person.

Alex sent one kid tumbling over backward and as he started to stand back up, Hillary let go with her best pitch. The rock hit the boy square on the forehead, and he groaned, sinking back to the ground. Alex took care of the other kid with one last stinging blow to the jaw.

He fell to the ground just as a blur of flashing lights turned the corner, followed by sirens. Within minutes, two police cars had pulled up alongside.

Alex walked over to Hillary and slid a hand around her trembling shoulders. "Nice pitch, sweetheart."

Hillary tried to smile, but now that the danger was over, she felt weak and dizzy. Her discomfort was aggravated by the blood smeared across Alex's lip. She instinctively raised a finger to touch his mouth, a tender, gentle, sorrowful gesture.

Alex tensed and caught her hand. "It's okay. I'm okay."

"You're hurt."

"Not bad. He looks worse." Alex motioned to the kid who was being helped into the police car by one of the officers. "I need to tell them what happened. Why don't you get in the car with Rocky."

Hillary nodded but didn't move as the officers took down his statement. When they turned to her, she was still standing on the sidewalk, staring at a slash of blood on the pavement.

"Hillary, they want to ask you a few questions."

She looked up. "Of course."

By the time she had run through the brief sequence of events, Hillary felt calmer. Finally the police took the youths down to the station and the three were free to go. She slid into the passenger seat and Alex got in behind the wheel. For a long moment the three of them just sat there, not looking at each other, not saying anything.

Rocky was the first to speak, and his voice came out small and hushed. "I'm sorry."

Alex sighed, leaning heavily on the steering wheel. "It's all right. You won't make that mistake again, I hope."

"No." Rocky bounced forward from the back seat. "But you were awesome. Where did you learn to fight like that?" Rocky moved his fists in a punching manner.

Alex sent Hillary a wry look and then started to grin. "Micky would be proud. I still have a good right jab." He lifted his hand and then winced in pain.

Hillary started at the motion, suddenly realizing the angle at which he was holding his wrist. "You're hurt, Alex. My God, your hand looks like it's broken."

"It kind of feels that way, too," he muttered.

"Get out. I'll drive," she ordered.

"I can do it."

"No, you can't. Stop being macho and move." Hillary opened her door and got out, walking around to Alex's side of the car. Once they were resettled in their seats, she turned to him. "How do I get to the nearest hospital?"

"I don't need a hospital."

"Yes, you do. You might need X rays or a cast."

"It looks bad," Rocky added.

"Yeah, what do you know?"

Hillary shook her head and pulled the car into traffic. As she recalled, there was a hospital just a few blocks away.

"You sure wrapped those dudes," Rocky commented. "I couldn't believe it. When I saw that knife I thought you were dead meat."

"Thanks for the vote of confidence."

"That's when I called the cops."

Hillary looked at Alex and they both started to laugh. "Smart kid," Alex said. "Maybe I'm glad you didn't have confidence in me. But I can take care of myself."

"Did you really train with Micky?" Hillary asked.

"For a while when I was younger. Now I just go for the workout. I don't use my fists much anymore. I try to use my brain, which is what you should be doing," he said to Rocky. "Why did you run away? You still haven't told me."

Rocky sat back against his seat with a grumpy frown. "I was practicing my driving in the Jenkinses' driveway. If the stupid cat hadn't run in front of me, I wouldn't have hit the garage door."

"You hit their garage door?" Alex demanded.

"Actually, I drove through it."

"What is wrong with you?" Alex shifted in his seat. "The Jenkinses are good foster parents. You don't know how lucky you are. I've been in places where they don't give a damn about the kids except to care how much money they get from the state."

"They were going to ground me," Rocky complained.

"Good. That means they care about you."

Hillary followed their conversation thoughtfully, wondering what Alex was talking about and why it sounded as though he was speaking from personal experience. But it wasn't the right time to break into their conversation, and besides, they were at the hospital. She pulled into the parking lot in front of the emergency entrance and turned off the engine.

"I'll go in by myself," Alex said. "Stay in the car with Rocky, and this time I mean stay in the car. Got it?"

"Yes, sir."

Alex rolled his eyes and got out of the car, pausing as Hillary turned to Rocky and said, "Looks like you and I will have time for a long chat."

He shook a warning finger at her, but Hillary ignored him. "Go get your hand fixed, Alex, we'll be fine."

Hillary was probably pumping the kid for information on him, Alex thought as the nurse stuck a needle deep into his arm, blending an immediate shaft of pain with blessed numbing relief. He tried to remember just what Rocky knew about him, and decided it wasn't much. Although he had made that slip about being in a foster home. Maybe Hillary had been too caught up in her driving to notice. If not, he'd have to make up some story to explain it. Maybe suggest that he'd spent a lot of time checking out foster homes for the kids who went to Micky's gym. Yes, that should hold her over.

His lips twisted with pain as the nurse jerked his arm into an uncomfortable position for the X rays. The pain almost felt like an appropriate punishment for the lies he was telling. Someday it was going to catch up to him. In fact, it already was. He was getting weary of the storytelling, especially around Hillary. She was so honest and forthright, upfront in her intentions; it seemed almost a sacrilege to bury the truth in front of those big blue eyes.

He stared at the white wall in front of him and then closed his eyes, aware that his emotions were coming very close to the surface, long, deeply buried emotions that he had never wanted to feel again. When that kid had terrorized Hillary, he had been filled with an almost uncontrollable rage to do some major bodily damage. If the police hadn't come along, he might not have been responsible for his actions. No one would hurt Hillary when he was around. No one.

The intensity of his feelings for her was staggering. He couldn't remember anyone in his life having such an impact on him. Oh, he would go to bat for his friends, always there to help out if he could, but he had never wanted to kill anyone before. Then it hit him, the depth of his rage and the depth of his love.

No, he wouldn't allow that word into his vocabulary. He did not love Hillary Blaine. He didn't even want to like her. Maybe a quick tumble in bed would be okay, but that was it. Nothing else. He couldn't afford to be that vulnerable again, to be that powerless, trussed up by his own feelings.

Just stay cool, he told himself. Finish the story and get her out of your life with no further harm done.

By the time his wrist was set in a cast and he was released from the hospital, nearly two hours had passed, and it was almost midnight. When he got to the car, Rocky was asleep in the back and Hillary was listening to some music on the stereo. She flipped the locks on the door so he could get in.

He tried not to look at her, not wanting to let any of his hard-built resolutions of the past two hours get tarnished by a tender look, a caressing hand.

But when Hillary touched the side of his face, tracing the bruise by his eye, his good hand went up to catch hers and he found himself letting her continue the gentle movement rather than pushing her away.

"My hero," she said softly with a gentle smile.

"Hardly. I almost got you killed."

Hillary laughed. "You're being polite now. I'm the one who got out of the car without thinking. I should have called 911 like Rocky did. Then you wouldn't be hurt."

"Why did you get out of the car in the first place?"

"I wanted to warn you."

"Even though you knew you could be in danger?"

Hillary flushed. "I didn't really think about it."

"You just hurtled yourself out of the car like an avenging angel." Alex smiled slowly. "I suppose you'd do that for anyone."

"I suppose. How's your hand? Is it broken?"

"Fractured."

"I'm sorry."

"It wasn't your fault. Shall we go home?"

"What about Rocky?"

Alex looked at Rocky sleeping peacefully in the back seat. "He can stay at my place tonight. I already called Mr. Jenkins."

Hillary nodded and started the car, backing out of the parking space with care. The last thing they needed was another accident. Alex settled back against his seat with a weary sigh, and she sneaked a quick look at him, wondering if he was in pain.

"Did they give you any medication?" she asked.

"A painkiller." Alex stifled a yawn. "I think it's working. Do you remember how to get to my house?"

"I think so."

"Good, I have a feeling I might drift away before we get there." He closed his eyes.

"Just relax, Alex. I'll get us home in one piece." Without thinking, she reached out a hand and patted his thigh. Alex slid his hand over hers, catching it in a warm, intimate grip, and he didn't let it go, not until the pain medication had him asleep.

During the quiet drive home, Hillary was filled with mixed emotions. The evening had not turned out as she had planned. They hadn't talked, hadn't done any work on the article. In fact, they'd missed dinner entirely, but she no longer was hungry. There was a hole in her stomach of another kind, a different ache that would not be appeased by food. She wanted to hold Alex in her arms and never let him go.

It was stupid to feel such a protectiveness toward the man. He had already proved he was more than capable of taking care of himself and whoever else needed a helping hand. But right now he looked vulnerable. His tie was open, hanging in two dangling ends down a white shirt that was now covered with dirt and blood. The bruise around his eye was puffy and angry looking and his hand looked as fat as a watermelon in a white cast.

A touch of guilt swept through her, even though she tried to push it aside. This was not her fault. She hadn't put Alex in a bad situation, Rocky's phone call had done that. Maybe her impulsiveness had created more problems, but that hadn't been her intention. Unfortunately trouble seemed to be her shadow.

What was supposed to be a routine celebrity profile was turning into a complicated mess. She was getting personally involved with a man who attracted her on many different levels, not just physically. His compassion for others touched a chord deep within her, and she had a feeling that he shared some of her loneliness, her isolation from the rest of the world.

Jogging with him in the park and watching the airplanes take off had put them in tune. On some deep level they understood each other. If only there was trust to go along with it.

But Alex didn't trust her. He had lied to her, and it was that fact she should be reminding herself of. He was a man with secrets, and it was her job to uncover them no matter what the cost, to Alex or to herself.

Her mind continued to wrestle with the situation, and it wasn't until she pulled into Alex's driveway that she realized she had other problems to consider. She had no transportation home, and both Alex and Rocky were asleep.

One thing at a time, she decided. After flipping through Alex's keys, she came across the house key and let herself in. Turning on the lights, she ventured upstairs, trying to get a handle on the layout of the house before she tried to get the other two inside.

There were six doors off the upstairs main hall and one by one she opened them. The first two were obviously guest rooms decorated in neutral colors with nothing in the way of personal furnishings. The third room was a girlish dream with white lace and pink bunny rabbits. Hillary stared in puzzlement at the contents. Alex lived alone and supposedly had no relatives. Who on earth stayed in this room?

Rocky would have been a choice, but her mind balked at that equation. There was no way a street kid like him would be caught dead in this room. Another piece of a very complicated puzzle that somehow made up Alex Donovan. Shaking her head in bewilderment, she closed the door and moved on to the next room.

It was a warm, comfortable study. There were bookshelves lining the walls and magazines spread out on the coffee table in front of a large overstuffed leather couch. There was a coffee cup by the phone and an open CD box by the stereo. She had finally found Alex's real home. She took a couple of steps inside and then put a halt on her curiosity. Exploring would have to wait for another time. She still had to find Alex's bedroom and somehow get him there.

With two more doors to go, she found another guest room and the master bedroom. The large suite was impressive in size and decor. A king-size bed was the focus of the room, with matching oak dresser and nightstands. There was an entertainment center on one wall and a large bay window with accompanying window seat. Hillary paused in the doorway, picturing Alex in the bed, walking out of the bathroom with a towel wrapped around his hips, his chest bare, with beads of water from a recent shower. He would smile at her and reach out. She would go into his arms and—

"Stop it, Hillary. You're losing it." It was time to get Rocky out of the car and get Alex into bed—alone.

When she got back to the car, she opened the door and shook Rocky gently on the shoulder. The boy stirred, blinking his eyes at her without any recognition.

"We're at Alex's house," she said reassuringly. "You can spend the night here. Can you get out on your own?"

Rocky nodded, yawning widely as he took off his seat belt. When he stepped out onto the driveway, the cool night air seemed to revive him and he looked back at Alex. "What about him?"

Hillary shrugged indecisively. "I suppose I could just let him sleep here. I know I can't carry him."

"He doesn't look very comfortable."

No, he didn't, not with his head propped at that awkward angle, and his right hand held protectively in his lap. If he moved and hit the door, he could very well hurt himself again.

"Maybe we could help him into the house together," Rocky suggested.

"You think so?"

Rocky nodded with the confidence of a twelve-year-old. "Sure." He yanked opened Alex's car door and yelled, "Alex, wake up."

Hillary rolled her eyes. "I could have done that."

Rocky grinned unapologetically and patted Alex on the shoulder. "Come on, wake up."

Alex groaned but didn't open his eyes.

"He's on pain medication." Hillary walked around the car. "Maybe if we each take a side, we can get him on his feet."

With quite a bit of maneuvering, they were finally able to get Alex out of the car and into the house. By the time they reached the stairs, he was awake enough to assist them, but whatever he was saying didn't make much sense. Finally they got to his bedroom, pushing him back onto the bed with a mutual sigh of relief. Alex promptly closed his eyes and began to snore.

Hillary looked at Rocky and grinned. "I think he's out."

"He doesn't look so good, does he?" Rocky said, with a touch of guilt coloring his voice.

"Don't feel bad. It wasn't your fault."

"Yes, it was. If I hadn't called him, he wouldn't have come. I should have just taken the bus to San Jose."

"And what would you have done there?"

"Find a place to hang out."

"Alex would have been pretty worried about you." Hillary kept her voice deliberately casual.

"Yeah, maybe."

"You two are pretty good friends, aren't you?"

"He's cool."

And that seemed to say it for him, Hillary thought with a kind smile. To Rocky, he was cool. To her, he was hot. Funny, how one man could engender two completely different emotions. She patted Rocky on the shoulder. "You must be tired. Why don't you go to bed?"

Rocky nodded and shuffled out of the room. Hillary stared down at Alex for a long moment. He didn't look very comfortable in his clothes, but there was no way she was going to attempt to undress him. She could at least take off his shoes though, maybe his tie so he didn't strangle himself.

The shoes came off with no problem. The tie slipped off his neck, and she managed to undo the buttons of his shirt without any problem. When she got to his waist, she pulled the ends of his shirt out of his pants. The belt was a bit more of a challenge. She released the buckle and started to pull it through the loops, but Alex moved, his shirt coming completely open, and she was staring at his solid, tanned chest. There was a smattering of dark hair covering the well-defined muscles of his chest and stomach, disappearing in a line below his waistband.

She flushed as her imagination completed the picture. What on earth was wrong with her? She had seen naked men before. The human body was certainly no mystery, so why did this half-dressed man send her pulses racing?

Her fingers lingered on his belt buckle as her eyes traveled up his chest, to the strong jaw, the generous curve of his mouth, the amused grin in his eyes, the spark of desire. Oh, Lord, he was awake.

"Are you taking off my pants?" His voice was calm and matter of fact, and Hillary suddenly realized that her fingers were playing with the snap on his waistband.

"I was just getting your belt off, to make you more comfortable, so you could sleep." She started to move, but Alex shifted, and his good hand came around her back, pulling her down on top of him.

The amusement in Alex's eyes faded into something darker and more dangerous.

"Hillary," he murmured, the quietness of his voice turning her name into an intimate caress. "I've dreamed of seeing you like this. Your hair falling down, brushing my face."

She stared at him, mesmerized by his tone, the hungry look in his eyes, the pulse working a rapid beat in his neck. She didn't resist when he pulled her face down to his. She was helpless, a victim of her own desire. He kissed her deeply, passionately, sliding his tongue into her mouth, demanding a response at the same time his hand ran down the length of her spine, making her arch like a cat.

He wasn't holding her anymore, but she just couldn't move. She couldn't deny the need that had been building inside her for days. Just one more kiss, one more moment, maybe two, and then she would stop. She would back away. She would pretend it had never happened.

But his mouth was working magic, his body stiffening against hers, making her aware of how fast they were moving, how intimate their position. She braced herself on her hands and slowly pulled away, her breath coming in ragged gasps.

Alex stared at her. "Don't go, Hillary. Stay with me."

"I can't," she whispered.

There was a light in his eyes, almost a fever. It burned right through her, tempting her, making her want to forget everything but the desire that was pulling them together.

"Need you," he murmured.

Hillary licked her lips. She wanted to believe him, but he was half-asleep, drugged by the medication.

"You don't know what you're saying." She sat back on her knees, looking down at him. He dropped his hand from her hair to his side, a look of pain turning his light green eyes to jade.

"Don't like me, do you?" His words were a mumble, and she had to lean down to hear them. "Sorry. Tried to be what you wanted. Not good enough. Never good enough."

"Alex, shh-shh." She placed her finger on his lips to quiet him, to stop whatever was upsetting him, but he merely kissed it, putting goose bumps down her arms.

"Don't leave me. Don't go. Can't take it anymore." His eyes drifted closed, and his breathing changed to one of slumber.

Hillary stared at him for a long moment, the anguish in his voice hitting her hard. Someone had hurt this man, hurt him badly. She rolled over onto her side, propping her head on her elbow as she stared at him. Impulsively, she reached out a finger and traced his lips, the strong cheekbones, the thick eyebrows that framed his brilliant eyes.

He was a good person. Instinctively she knew that, even though a part of her conscience screamed that he had lied to her. She didn't know why he hadn't been honest, or what game he was playing, but she wanted to believe that he had a good reason, that it had something to do with the torment in his voice.

Slipping off her shoes, Hillary shifted position and put one hand under her head like a pillow, the other resting lightly on Alex's waist. It was a little chilly in the room in spite of her sweater, so she pulled up a quilt from the bottom of the bed and covered them both. She would just stay with him for a little while. In case his hand hurt, and he needed something, she told herself. It would never do for him to wake up and find her nestled against his side. He would get the wrong idea, she thought sleepily, closing her eyes as the lemon scent of his after-shave covered her with warmth. Just a few minutes...

Chapter Ten

The sunlight streaming through the window drew Alex out of a deep slumber. When he tried to move, he felt bruised and stiff and heavy, as if there was a large weight on his chest. He blinked one eye open and then the other, and then blinked again, unable to believe what he was seeing.

His other senses immediately clicked in. Blond hair tickled the bare skin on his chest. A slender leg intertwined with his, causing an immediate reaction in another part of his body.

Good grief. Hillary was in bed with him. It had to be a dream—a bright, vivid dream. He could smell the scent of her shampoo, see the dark lashes curving down against her cheek, her expression as innocent as a baby's.

He shook his head and closed his eyes again, but when he took another look she was still there. A heavy fog filled his mind as he tried to make sense of the obvious. They had gone to bed together, and he didn't remember a damn thing. But something was wrong.

He groaned as he moved his right arm, and the memories of the past evening came flooding back. He remembered getting into the car after leaving the hospital and that was it.

Somehow Hillary and Rocky must have dragged him into the house and up the stairs. But that didn't explain why she had gotten into bed with him, why she had slept with him instead of going home or just using one of the guest rooms.

He shifted slightly, hoping she wouldn't wake up. Now that he was awake and alert, he wanted to take a better look.

Asleep, Hillary looked a lot softer, untouched by the harsh side of life. Her skin was clear and smooth with just a few laugh lines around the corners of her eyes. He smiled tenderly, thinking of her open, charming grin, the laughter that would reach her eyes, even when she tried to be serious. She was still wearing the deep turquoise blue dress from the night before, but it had ridden high on her legs, revealing the curve of tantalizing thighs.

She would hate the fact that he was watching her, seeing her off guard without all her defenses in place. He smiled to himself, enjoying the way her arm curved around his waist. It felt good, too damn good. He didn't want her to wake up. He wanted her to hold him forever. But even as the thought came to mind, she gently began to stir, waking up in slow, uneasy stages that brought indistinguishable murmurs to her lips.

He liked the way she fought off the morning. It was in keeping with the way she resisted him, an inevitable futile struggle against what was meant to be.

Finally, Hillary's eyes opened, and she stared at him, at first blankly, and then with a dawning sense of awareness and embarrassment. She raised her head and took a quick look down her body, immediately reaching to smooth out her dress. Then she pushed herself into a half-sitting position, her hair falling down, a curtain against her expression.

He reached up and pushed her hair back behind her ear, so he could see her face. "Good morning, sunshine. I'm glad you finally decided to sleep with me."

"I didn't. I mean—" she paused "—you're awake."

"Very good. So are you."

She looked around in confusion. "You're probably wondering what I'm doing here."

He propped himself up on the pillows and patted her knee. "Actually, I'm just hoping you'll stay. No questions asked. At least until you've kissed me good morning."

"I'm not going to kiss you good morning."

"It's customary when two people go to bed together."

"We didn't go to bed together."

"This is my bed. We're both in it."

Hillary swallowed hard, trying to get her wits about her. The first thing she needed to do was get off the damn bed. But Alex's good hand was now clenched firmly around her wrist, prohibiting a quick escape.

"Not so fast."

"How's your hand?" she asked, trying to distract him.

"It needs some T.L.C, a good-morning kiss."

"I doubt that a kiss is going to heal your fracture."

"But it would do wonders for other parts of my anatomy."

Hillary looked away from the twinkle in his eye, unwilling to think about those other parts. As it was, she was having trouble thinking at all. His clothes were rumpled. He needed a shave and the bruise over his eye had turned a hideous shade of purple, but he still looked good. She took in a deep breath and slowly let it out.

In the bright light of day, it was difficult to believe that his voice had held such pain, that his need for comfort had seemed so strong. Now he was back to being self-assured and on top of the world, and she was once again off balance. Completely off balance, she thought as he pulled her on top of him.

"Alex, don't."

"One kiss, and then you can go."

"It won't stop there."

"It will if you want it to."

She hesitated, staring hard at his face. He wasn't lying. He would let her go. The problem was with herself. She might not want to let go.

"Kiss me, Hillary." Alex shut his eyes, waiting for her to take the initiative.

He seemed harmless for a moment, and so she pressed her lips to his, tentatively, and then more firmly. She suddenly wanted to be able to arouse him as easily and as quickly as he did her. She ran her tongue lightly against his lips, rejoicing in the low groan that came from his now parted lips. She traced her mouth around the corners of his, teasing him until she was caught in her own trap, wanting nothing more than a deep possession of his mouth and his body.

A door slammed down the hall, and she jolted upright, sending a panic-stricken look at Alex's bedroom door, but it was still closed—for the moment.

"Rocky," she said.

"It's okay. He won't come in, not without knocking."

She swallowed hard. "I have to go. I can't imagine what he would think if he saw me in here."

"He'd probably think that we were making love. He's a smart kid. He knows there's something going on between us—even if you don't."

Hillary shot him a confused look and then slid off the bed, this time without meeting any resistance from Alex. She stumbled around for her shoes, finding one half-hidden under the bed. When she finally had them both on, she looked over at Alex, who was watching her with an unreadable expression on his face.

"I'll make us some coffee, okay?"

He nodded slowly. "Whatever makes you happy."

"Alex, don't . . ."

"Don't what?"

"I stayed with you last night because I was worried about you. I thought you might wake up and be in pain." It was partly the truth, although for some reason she found herself strangely reluctant to tell him the rest, that she had found his words disturbing, and that he had shown a part of himself to her that she hadn't known existed.

"And you would have done that for anyone," he said flatly, his eyes losing some of their sparkle.

"For a friend, yes." She fiddled with a piece of lint on her sweater, not wanting to look into his eyes, afraid of what she would see there.

"A friend." He uttered a short, harsh laugh. "That's something I suppose."

"Do you want some coffee?" Hillary asked, desperate to get things back on an impersonal track, which was going to be impossible if she didn't get out of his bedroom.

"Sure, why not." He sat up and swung his legs off the side of the bed, unable to repress a murmur of pain as he did so.

Hillary hesitated. "Are you okay, Alex? Do you want me to get you some of your medication?"

He shook his head. "No. The last thing I need is to be unconscious. Who knows what you'll get up to."

"I wouldn't take advantage of you like that."

"You already did, by sleeping with me when I was too weak to do anything about it."

"I was taking care of you. You should be grateful."

He took a deep breath and stood up, swaying for a moment. "Maybe I'll be able to appreciate your true motives after I take a shower."

"I don't think that's a good idea. You're not too steady on your feet right now."

"Don't worry, I'll be okay. Just see if you can get some coffee going and check in on Rocky. That kid's got an appetite. He's probably cleaning out my cupboards right now."

Hillary walked to the door and paused, torn between wanting to help Alex and wanting to get as far away from him as possible. Alex looked up and saw her watching him. He shook his head at her unspoken question.

"You better leave now, Hillary, before you change your mind—" he paused, the air crackling with tension "—or I change it for you."

Hillary took the stairs two at a time, jogging down to the first floor as if the devil were after her. And maybe he was. Alex had a way of bringing out her wild side and to heck with her conscience.

Rocky was eating a bowl of cereal at the kitchen counter and watching cartoons on the television. He looked up when she walked in, his face turning wary and guarded.

She smiled. "Morning. I see you got something to eat."

"Alex always says to help myself."

"Then I guess it's a good thing that you did." She walked around the island in the kitchen and stared at the clean, granite-topped counters. Somewhere in the mass of cabinets was a coffeemaker and probably some food, but where?

Rocky pointed to a cupboard by the refrigerator. "Cereal's in there if you want some."

"Thanks, but I was looking for a coffeemaker."

"Over there." Rocky motioned to the other side of the room and Hillary followed his instructions to find the most complicated-looking coffeepot she had ever seen in her life. It was nothing like the one at work that you filled with water, plugged in, and turned on. This one had different settings and shades, and more buttons than she'd seen on a computer.

"It figures," she mumbled to herself, eyeing the thing with a grouchy frown. "Alex Donovan would have to have the deluxe coffeemaker. Too bad, you can't talk."

After pulling the coffeemaker out of the cabinet, she plugged it in and stared hard at the various points of instruction. Inside the cabinet she found coffee beans and a grinder.

Hillary was nothing if not independent and determined. She was not about to let a little thing like making coffee get her down. After guessing at the instructions, grinding the beans and filling the cup with water, she turned it on and stood back, waiting for the first sizzle. The opening drops looked promising, a dark, rich brown in color. As the pot began to fill, a pleasant aroma filled the room. She had done it. She had made coffee.

With a triumphant smile, she walked over to the refrigerator and examined the contents like a general overseeing the troops. Eggs, milk, butter. She could definitely handle scrambled, maybe some toast. And there was always cereal.

By the time Alex came down the stairs, she had breakfast almost ready and was pleasantly awaiting his surprised expression. She might be a hard-boiled reporter, but she did have a few domestic capabilities. Not that she was trying to impress him. She had never bought into her mother's theory that any man worth having was worth cooking for. Still, it would be nice to know she could do it if she wanted to.

And for some reason she did want to. Alex was not only bringing out her repressed sexuality, he was also making her examine other parts of her life, her tunnel vision toward work and her obsession with moving on before she even had time to appreciate what she already had.

"Smells good," Alex commented, sniffing the air with a surprised expression.

She smiled, a mix of delight and rueful tenderness as her gaze swept over his black eye. "How's your face?"

Alex touched the tip of his eye with his finger. "It feels as bad as it looks, and it's been a long time since I had one of these. Is the coffee ready yet?"

Hillary's smile faded as she looked over at the pot. It had definitely stopped perking, and the pot was full. Might as well go for broke. She reached for the cup and saucer she had pulled out of the cabinet and poured him some coffee. "Do you want cream or sugar?"

"No, I like it black."

Alex accepted the coffee cup from her hand with a grateful smile and took a sip. The liquid came right back out of his mouth with a spitting grimace, sending drips of coffee all over the counter.

Hillary looked at him in astonishment.

"This—this is horrible." He stared down at the cup as if she had offered him poison.

"It is?" she asked tentatively.

He handed her the cup. "Take a sip."

She reluctantly accepted it, putting her lips on the rim. After seeing Alex's display, she allowed only a small portion into her mouth, immediately gagging at the thick, chunky quality of the liquid. He was right. It was ghastly.

"If you had a normal coffeepot, like a normal person, I would have been fine, but these sixty-million-dollar gadgets are a little beyond my experience," she replied.

"So this is my fault." He shook his head in amazement. "Why don't you just admit that you can't make coffee? Did you even attempt to grind the beans?"

"Of course I did. And I can make coffee. I just can't make it in your house."

"Hillary, the eggs..." Rocky's voice cut into their argument, and Hillary looked over at the stove where her scrambled eggs were now smoking and turning black.

She threw up her hands. "Great, now look what you did."

"Me? My fault, again?"

Hillary ran out of the kitchen, feeling a tremendous urge to cry her eyes out. She couldn't do anything right. She was hopeless, a complete failure as a woman. Her mother was right. The things men cared about, she just couldn't do. There was no point in pretending otherwise.

Once she was in the hall, she paused, unsure of where to go. She had to get her purse, but she still didn't have a car, so she would either have to call for a cab or go back in and face Alex.

"Hillary?" Alex walked out of the kitchen and paused halfway down the hall, giving her plenty of space. "I'm sorry."

She shook her head in denial. "Why? You were only telling the truth. I should be apologizing to you for messing up your coffee and burning your breakfast."

"I don't like eggs, anyway." He gave her a coaxing smile.

"You're just saying that."

"No, I'm not. And I don't care that you can't cook. You have a lot of other nice qualities."

"Sure I do."

"I can't think of one woman I know who would have thrown a rock at a mugger to protect me, or danced in the middle of a street under a full moon."

His tender words made her drop her gaze, and she stared down at the dark shades of wood on the floor. "It was no big deal, the rock, I mean," she said. "The dancing was your idea."

"I'd be happy to make you coffee if you'll stay for a while."

Her head perked up. "Why are you being so nice to me?"

"Maybe I'm just returning the favor. Some women would have walked out on me and Rocky last night, but you stayed for the long haul." He paused, luring her with an enticing smile. "I make great pancakes. But I need an extra hand. Maybe together, we can do the job."

"You'd probably do better with one hand than I could with two." She offered him a reluctant smile and took a few steps in his direction.

He held out his good hand, waiting for her to take it. In the ten seconds that it took for her to move down the hall, Hillary felt as though something had changed between them. It wasn't anything concrete or clear-cut, just an indefinable feeling of mutual understanding.

They walked back toward the kitchen, hand in hand. "I think I could get used to your being my better half," he said.

Hillary's stomach turned over at the warm words, and she murmured something inaudible as she pulled her hand away from his and pushed open the kitchen door. The blaring sound of the television set put an end to their private conversation.

"How about a big stack of hotcakes, Rocky?" Alex asked.

Rocky looked from one to the other. "Who's cooking?"

Hillary made a face and pointed at Alex. "He is."

"Count me in."

Alex laughed as he smiled over at Hillary. "What about you? Are you with me?"

She nodded, knowing her answer extended to more than just pancakes. But she would deal with that problem later.

Breakfast turned out to be a comfortable meal with delicious pancakes topped with creamy butter and maple syrup. Fresh-squeezed orange juice and strong, hot coffee also helped take the edge off the morning. Hillary enjoyed listening to the banter between Rocky and Alex and realized that these men, one full-grown, and one half-size, shared a mutual respect for each other.

Unfortunately, when she attempted to get some personal history, she felt like a deep-sea diver going after a pearl in an oyster. Every time she got close, the shell snapped shut.

"Do you want some more pancakes, Hillary?" Alex asked, catching her staring at his plate and misinterpreting her thoughts. "Because if you think you're going to get my last bite, you're crazy."

Hillary smiled, thinking back to the first dinner they had shared. "I wouldn't dream of trespassing on someone else's breakfast."

"Alex hates to share," Rocky interjected with a broad-faced grin. "He won't even give me a handful of popcorn out of his carton when we go to the movies. He always makes me get my own."

"So you get enough," Alex replied, his lips turning down into a frown. "I don't think my eating habits need to be discussed in such great detail."

Hillary rested her elbows on the table. "Why the big deal about food, Alex? Is that some primitive territorial urge?"

Alex rolled his eyes. "No, it's some primitive, feed-my-hunger urge."

"You act like you're afraid you won't get enough, but since you can buy an entire supermarket, I hardly think you have to worry."

"I don't take my life-style for granted. Things can change at any moment."

She looked at him thoughtfully. "You think your money could disappear in a day?"

"Your whole life can disappear in a second." He snapped his fingers. "Nothing is for sure. Nothing is forever."

"Not even love?" she whispered softly.

"That's the most illusory thing of all."

"Maybe. Maybe not. I'm beginning to think some things just won't go away, no matter how much you want them to."

Alex took another bite of his pancake and nodded. "You might be right about that. But food is not one of them, especially when Rocky is around. He can clean out my cupboard in two minutes."

"One minute, thirty seconds," Rocky retorted.

Hillary smiled. "Okay, enough with the food question. I have another one."

Alex groaned. "You always have another question."

"Who uses the pink-and-white bedroom upstairs?"

Rocky let out a somber "Uh-oh" and slid his chair back from the table. "I think I'll go play a video game."

"What did I say?" she asked.

"You snooped around my house? When? Last night when I was sound asleep?"

Hillary shifted in her chair. "I was looking for your bedroom, Alex. Don't blow it out of proportion."

He raised his orange-juice glass to his lips and took a long drink. By the time he set it down on the table, Hillary was as tense as a finely strung guitar.

"What is the matter?" she demanded, ignoring her inner call for patience. "You act like I just found a dead body in the basement."

"That room is off limits."

"Why? It's beautiful. I bet there are dozens of little girls who would die to sleep on that white feather bed."

"It was furnished for someone I thought might be coming, but she didn't. I'm going to have it redone as soon as I have a chance. After all, there's no point in a bachelor having a room like that." Alex stared down at the maple syrup on his plate, taking one finger and wiping it along the edge and then licking it off his finger.

"Then what's the big deal?"

He looked up at her and smiled. "No big deal. You asked. I answered. End of story. Next question, please."

Hillary sighed and inwardly gave up. The standard interview was not going to work with Alex. He revealed much more through his actions and relationships with other people than he did through oblique answers to her questions.

"Hillary?"

She lifted her empty plate. "Can I have some more pancakes?"

By the end of the next week, Hillary had discovered a few more truths about Alex. He was very neat and organized. He lived simply and he ate well. The refrigerator and cupboard were always well stocked with hearty, healthy foods. He ran every morning, even with his wrist in a sling, and he had his own exercise room in the basement.

Although she spent her nights at home, she spent most of the day with Alex, and usually Rocky when he came by after school. She told herself that she was simply doing her job and also helping Alex maneuver around the house with his bad hand, but in fact, she was enjoying herself immensely.

Being with Rocky and Alex made her feel part of a family again, and she hadn't felt that way in a long time. She walked out of Alex's kitchen and pulled open the curtains over the family room windows. Alex and Rocky were piling a stack of wood in the backyard, laughing and gesturing with their hands about some new project. She smiled to herself, wondering what they were going to get into now. Not that she was much better at averting disasters. After a few miserable efforts at cooking, she had given up trying to be the happy homemaker and was content to help Alex, who had turned out to be quite an excellent chef.

It was strange how everything she had learned about men from her mother and sister had prepared her to play out a certain role, but with Alex, the lines dimmed. His Cornish game hen was superb, but he couldn't fix the washer on the sink to save his life, and when Hillary pulled out the tools and went to work he simply stood back and applauded.

He also respected her privacy, her alone time. She didn't feel as though she had to talk to Alex all the time, entertain him with her wit or hover over him like a mother hen. He was self-reliant, and so was she.

As for love and affection, it was always there, simmering under the surface, threatening to boil over at unexpected times, and not necessarily in front of a fire with a glass of champagne. Just yesterday they had been throwing a football in the backyard and she had slipped on the grass. Alex had fallen down on top of her. That's when she had thought making love on a bed of grass had definite merits.

Unfortunately, the good times were coming to an end. The truce on her article had to come to a close. Making her way back to the kitchen, Hillary couldn't ignore the fact that she needed to write the story, and to do so, Alex was going to have to open up, and it didn't look as if he was going to do it of his own accord.

It made her sad and depressed that he didn't trust her enough to share the truth of his life. He was obviously still afraid of what she would do with the information. And maybe he had reason to be. She wasn't sure herself. Every time she walked into his home, she knew that she could never hurt him. But every time she walked into her newsroom cubicle, she knew that she might have to hurt him to fulfill the other need in her life to get ahead, to be somebody.

She looked up as the back door opened.

"Hi, sweetheart." Alex walked in, dressed in faded blue jeans with torn knees and a paint-spattered work shirt.

She grinned at him. "What are you dressed for? I thought we were going to take Rocky to the planetarium."

"Change in plans. Rocky has a science project due on Monday. Of course, he's had the assignment for three weeks, but he decided to start working on it today. So, in the next twenty-four hours, he has to come up with a brilliant idea."

"And he turned to you, what a coincidence."

Alex walked over to her and planted his hands on her shoulders, massaging the muscles in her neck. A shadow crossed his face as he looked down at her. "Does it bother you that I'm spending so much time with him? I want to make sure he feels okay with his foster parents, but at the same time I don't want him to feel I'm deserting him."

Hillary nodded, loving the compassion that made him feel so deeply for people. "I don't mind at all. But do you think you can manage with your hand?"

"I think so." He shot a look over his shoulder where Rocky was hammering a nail through a board. His hands drifted down the sides of her arms, to her waist, and he slipped his thumbs through the belt loops in her jeans. The action brought their hips into close contact, and the desire that was so carefully banked and controlled between them jerked into action.

"Rocky is waiting," Hillary reminded him, wishing her voice didn't sound so breathless and affected.

"So am I. We haven't been alone in a while." He leaned over and brushed her mouth with his.

"We're not alone now."

Alex smiled against her lips. "I can block him out if you can."

She laughed. "I don't think so."

"You're a tough lady."

Hillary stepped back at his words, the lightness in her soul turning heavy. Although she aspired to be tough, sometimes the definition bothered her. It made her sound so unfeminine, so unlovable.

"That was a compliment," Alex said, dropping a kiss on the tip of her nose.

"Really? I know I'm a lousy cook and a terrible housekeeper, and I hardly have any dresses in my closet."

Alex pulled her back into his arms, hugging her tightly. "Good, because I like you better without any clothes."

"You haven't seen me without any clothes."

"But I've imagined you."

Hillary laughed and hugged him back. "Fantasy is a long way from fact."

He looked down at her and winked. "Why don't you prove it? Put your money—or your body—where your mouth is."

"I don't have to prove anything, and I am not going to stand here and mess around with you when Rocky is in the backyard."

"Okay. Okay." Alex let her go. "Do you want to help?"

"Sure. I can swing a hammer, drill a hole."

Alex looked at her doubtfully. "Somehow the thought of a power tool in your hands is not something I want to contemplate."

"Very funny." Hillary gave him a push. "Go on outside. I'll be around." She hesitated and then spoke. "The article is not going to go away."

"I know. But tomorrow is Monday, and we'll get back to work." He turned the knob on the back door and then stopped. "Sometimes, I'd really like to drop this story."

"You made a commitment to the magazine."

"Yes, but that isn't the reason you don't want me to quit, is it? You need this article for your career."

"A cover story is always a plus," she admitted.

"So I'm a stepping stone on your way up the ladder. You'd probably crawl right over me if you had to."

"I'm not trying to destroy you. I have a job to do."

"This isn't just about the article. There's something going on between us."

"What? What?" she demanded, secretly hoping he would put it into words, laying everything out on the table for both of them. "What is this thing that's going on between us?"

Alex ran a hand through his hair, obviously uncomfortable with the direct question. "You know."

"But you can't say the words, can you? How strong can this *thing* be if you can't even put a name to it?" She waved her hand in frustration. "I can say I like you. I can even admit that I might be falling in love with you." Her words came out in a gush of emotion, and she almost took them back, but she knew how important it was for Alex to see where they were headed. If he wanted a straight, uncomplicated relationship, it was not going to be with her.

"Hillary." He reached out a hand, and then paused as Rocky called his name, and the moment of revelation was lost. "We'll talk later, okay?"

"Sure." She tucked her hair behind her ear and smiled cynically. "Later."

When he was gone, she let out a breath. That was great. She had just told her interview subject she was in love with him. Another smart move for Hillary Blaine. Shaking her head, she stared out the window at Rocky and Alex, wondering if she should join them or go home and try to get some perspective in her life.

With a cross expression on her face, she turned away from the window and walked over to the kitchen counter where her keys lay waiting invitingly. She had just picked them up when the phone rang. One last act of charity, she decided. She picked up the receiver and spoke. "Donovan residence."

"Is Alex there?" A woman's voice came over the wire faintly hesitant and unsure.

Hillary stiffened, wondering which woman this was. During the past week, she had overheard quite a few calls, constantly reminding her that if she didn't want this man, there were dozens of women who did.

"May I ask who's calling?" she said perversely, playing her fingers around the telephone cord.

"Do you know when he'll be back?" the woman countered.

"Shortly." Hillary took a look over her shoulder and decided not to interrupt. Alex could certainly take a call for a date in half an hour when she didn't have to listen to it. "Do you want me to take a message?"

"Yes. Tell Alex to meet me at Pier 39 tomorrow, in front of the card shop, at 2:00 p.m. I'll wait for an hour."

Hillary jotted down the message, a strange uneasiness entering into her mind. This didn't sound like the normal Alex Donovan groupie. The woman's voice was older, for one thing, and almost desperate, as if she didn't believe Alex would come.

"Who may I tell him called?" she asked again. "So that he'll understand the message."

The woman hesitated for a long moment. "His mother."

Chapter Eleven

Alex ran faster as his heart began to throb against his chest, and his breathing came in short, harsh gasps. The sweat was dripping down his face, and still he pushed himself to go faster, to ignore the pain in his wrist that grew worse with each movement of his arm. He had to get away, not only from Micky and his questions, but from Hillary. Even here, on a jog with his good friend, she was haunting his thoughts.

The pain in his side grew sharp and stabbing, and finally he slowed to a walk as he reached the end of the running path just underneath the Golden Gate Bridge. He leaned over the railing, staring down at the tumultuous blue-green water.

It fit his mood exactly. Gradually his breathing eased, and he straightened, willing himself to be comforted by the smell of salt in the air and the sounds of birds singing their way to the ocean. But it was no use. He couldn't think about anything but Hillary. The water reminded him of their first outing on the boat. Even seasick, Hillary had been feisty and honest. She had never lied to him. Maybe he didn't like what she had to say, but at least it had come from her heart and not from a pair of fake, painted lips. He closed his eyes, the memory of a long-ago day coming clearly into his mind. Maybe it was good to remember the pain. Then he wouldn't make the same mistakes again.

"I'll come back for you," she had said with such a convincing, tearful smile that he had believed her. She had made him promise not to cry, to be a big boy, and he had tried. No one ever saw his tears, but sometimes in the middle of the night, he would wake up and his pillowcase would be wet. After a while even those tears had stopped and he had grown a strong iron shell around his heart. She hadn't come back, and he told himself over and over again that he was glad.

He opened his eyes as a runner came to a stop next to him.

"If you wanted me to shut up, why didn't you just say so, instead of making me run a two-minute mile?" Micky grumbled, clutching his side with a painful frown. "I thought I was in shape, but not for the sprint you just pulled."

"Sorry. I just felt like moving."

"What did I say?" Micky asked.

"Nothing."

"I said Hillary, and your body went into overdrive."

Alex shook his head. "It had nothing to do with her."

"Yeah, right." Micky paused. "Are you going to work this morning or are you spending the day with her?"

"Work. She left yesterday, didn't even say goodbye. I guess she got sick of me and Rocky."

"Did you make her mad or something?"

Alex stretched out his back leg until he could feel the hamstring tighten and then did the same with the other leg as he thought about Micky's question. "No, I did not make her mad, at least not that I know of, although she goes off faster than a firecracker." Alex straightened. "Are you ready to go back?"

"No, I'm not ready. I just got here. Give me a break." He paused. "Besides, I want to know what's going on with the article. Has anything come to light?"

Alex shifted restlessly, Micky's words reinforcing his own doubts. "I don't think so, but sometimes I see Hillary looking at me with a strange expression in her eyes. And then her walking out yesterday didn't seem to make sense. I don't know. The intricacies of a woman's mind are beyond me."

"Maybe you should talk to her," Micky suggested, holding up a hand as Alex started to interrupt. "You can't hide forever. Sometimes I don't know why you even want to try."

"It's not for me. You know that." Alex stared into Micky's sharp blue eyes and saw the immediate perception.

"Right, I forgot. The kids."

"I won't take anyone else's innocence. I just won't do it."

"Maybe Hillary would—"

"Would what? Give up on the story? Her chance to make it to the big time? Do you really think she would do that?" Alex demanded. "She's obsessed with her career, and I've seen firsthand what that kind of obsession can do to a relationship."

Micky gave him a long, hard look. "Maybe you're confusing her with someone else."

"And maybe I'm not. I can't afford to make the same mistake. I don't think I could handle it twice."

Micky nodded, rubbing his forehead with the back of his arm. "It's a risk. I'll give you that. But sometimes you have to take a few punches to win the whole thing."

Alex looked away, feeling like a coward and a fool. He didn't want to take a punch. He was afraid he would be rejected again or that his trust would be abused. The smart, safe thing to do was get Hillary out of his life and to hell with the article and the free press. He could live without publicity and more business. The problem, was he didn't think he could live without Hillary.

This is wrong, Hillary thought as she stared across the street at Pier 39. *You should have told Alex about the phone call. You're invading his privacy, not doing your job.*

Looking indecisively at her watch, Hillary realized it was five minutes to two. Since she hadn't told Alex about the phone call, and since he obviously wasn't going to be coming, the woman was going to spend a futile hour waiting for him.

Taking a deep breath, Hillary left the parking structure and walked across the street. There were tourists weaving in and out of the shops along the pier, street artists doing mime for coins, and the ever constant smell of saltwater and seafood from Fisherman's Wharf. The card shop was the second one in, next to a hot dog snack bar, smelling of onions and mustard. Hillary stopped a good five feet from the entrance and looked around.

How on earth was she going to know who to talk to? There were people everywhere, and she had no idea what this woman looked like. Hillary turned around, the answer suddenly obvious. Standing next to a fountain was an older woman with dark black hair, a softer, feminine version of Alex. She was tall and slender, wearing a sophisticated rose-colored suit. She appeared to be somewhere in her early fifties, and obviously well-off judging by the large diamond ring on her third finger, the one she was tapping nervously against her purse.

Hillary took a deep breath and walked over to her. "Mrs. Donovan?"

The woman looked at her in confusion. "No."

"You're not Alex Donovan's mother?"

She looked at her warily. "Who are you?"

It wasn't an answer to her question, but at least they were talking. Hillary extended her hand in a friendly gesture. "Hillary Blaine. I think I spoke to you on the phone yesterday. You asked Alex to meet you here at two?"

The woman shook her hand, relief flooding her features. "Yes. Where is he?"

"I'm afraid he's not here." Hillary felt a rush of guilt at the pain in her eyes. She should have given Alex the message instead of trying to get some information on her own.

"I didn't really think he would be," the woman said dejectedly. "He hasn't come yet, not even after all my letters. When you answered the phone, I felt a renewed sense of hope. I thought maybe things had changed, that a woman in his life might be able to convince him to patch things up with me."

"I'm not the woman in his life," Hillary said. "And I shouldn't have come here. To be honest, I'm a reporter. I'm doing an article on Alex, and when you called, I couldn't believe the opportunity. Alex told me that you were dead, but obviously you're not." Her words came out in a rush and the woman stared at her in confusion.

"You're a reporter?"

"Yes."

The woman sighed and walked over to a stone bench by the fountain. She sat down and stared at her leather pumps. Hillary hesitated and then walked over to join her.

"I'm sorry for misleading you. I should have given him your message. But when I didn't, and I realized you'd be waiting, I thought it was better to just tell you the truth so you could call him again."

"Alex told you I was dead?" The woman's head lifted and her eyes filled with tears. "I thought maybe he would have dropped that story by now. I guess he just prefers to think of me in those terms. He can't forgive me, or maybe he won't."

She fell silent and for a moment the rush of water from the fountain mingling with the chatter of the crowds and a wailing child took precedence over their conversation.

Finally Hillary got to her feet. "I can only apologize again, and hope that I haven't messed things up for you."

The woman looked up at her. "How is he?"

"He's fine." Hillary shrugged, not sure she could respond adequately to the intensity of her simple question. "He's a very attractive, successful man, kind and compassionate. He's going to be Man of the Year in my magazine."

"And he's happy, really happy?"

"I don't know if I can answer that."

The woman nodded in understanding. "I suppose only Alex can answer that question. He had a very difficult life early on. You see, I—"

Hillary cut her off with a brisk shake of her head. "No, don't tell me. It's between you and Alex, and like I said, I don't really have any right to the information. I don't know why I intercepted his phone call. But I can't do this, not to Alex. I'm sorry." She stumbled over her words anxious to get away, to not do anything further to destroy Alex's faith in her.

The woman rose in a regal, dignified manner that masked some of her unhappiness. "You must care about him a great deal."

"I do. I mean, I don't. I mean, I don't know. We have a strange relationship." Hillary smiled. "I have to go."

The woman put a hand on her arm as she turned to leave. "Wait, will you give Alex a note?" She opened her purse and pulled out a white envelope. "I wrote it just in case he wouldn't stay long enough to talk to me."

Hillary took the envelope somewhat reluctantly, knowing that she had just sealed her fate. There would be no way now that she could pretend not to have seen Alex's mother. But it was the least she could do after botching everything else up. Once again, she had acted impetuously. She had to start thinking things through.

She slipped the note into her purse and walked hurriedly back to her car, not allowing herself to look back or to speculate about the woman in the fashion suit, the woman who was supposed to be dead, along with someone named Harold Donovan. And she hadn't even gotten her name. The only thing she knew was that she claimed to be Alex's mother, she looked just like him, and she wasn't Mrs. Donovan.

Alex picked up the phone in his office and buzzed the intercom. "Any answer at Hillary's, Rosemary?"

"No, sir. Her office says she's out all day, and her answering machine is picking up at home."

"Okay, thanks. Keep trying, would you?"

"Is she supposed to meet you?"

"No." His answer felt as bleak as it sounded, and he didn't really know why. Hillary and he had gotten very close over the past few days, maybe not physically, but definitely emotionally. The night she had slept in his arms had been a turning point for both of them. But somehow he felt things had changed again, and it was niggling at him like a painful tooth.

He stared at the receiver and belatedly hung it up. The work on his desk beckoned to him, but he couldn't bear to study the profit and loss statement. It certainly wasn't interesting enough to take his mind off Hillary.

Leaning over, he flipped the switch on the train and watched it begin its inevitable journey. Sometimes he felt as though he was riding the train, always on the same track, making the same turns, never able to break away, to venture into new ground, because this was the way the train had always gone, the way it would continue to go. Any change could lead to disaster, to accidents, to uncharted territory, to Hillary.

Maybe it was time to take a chance, set down new tracks, chart a new course. Fall in love. No, how could he? He didn't believe in love. It was an illusion created by the writers of bridal magazines and the bakers of wedding cakes.

How could two people become one, intimately in tune with each other's thoughts and emotions and bodies, without losing sight of who they were? And how could he bring someone into his life without telling them everything, without feeling the intense, hideous shame of his childhood. He wanted to forget about that part of his life, not rehash it with someone before he took them to bed. But Hillary would never be satisfied with only a part of his life. She would have to know everything.

In some ways, he could understand that feeling, because the more he knew about her, the more he wanted to know. He wanted to see pictures of her as a baby. He wanted to hear stories from her mother and sister, about the time she cut off her hair or got suspended from school for fighting with a boy. He wanted to know about the little girl who hated frilly dresses and adored a father who was constantly leaving. He wanted to get inside of her mind and her body, to share her joy, to ease her pain, to make her understand that she was gorgeous and sexy for who she was, not for what she wore.

He sat back in his chair, hearing the springs squeak with the change in his weight. He felt heavy and depressed. A gray cloud had darkened his sky when Hillary walked out. He knew something had happened. Something that would change his life.

The door opened, and he looked up, the haunting image in his mind coming to life in the doorway. Hillary paused uncertainly, as if unsure of her welcome. He felt exactly the same way. Suddenly they were two strangers, not the man and woman who had battled over Trivial Pursuit late into the night or shared a carton of cookie-dough ice cream for breakfast.

Hillary was the reporter again. She had on her game face, and he responded accordingly, sitting up straight in his chair, on guard, ready, he hoped, for anything.

"Hello, Alex. Rosemary said I could come in."

He nodded, his throat suddenly too tight to speak. He cleared it and reached over to shut off the train.

"Don't. I like to watch it go," Hillary said, stepping inside and closing the door behind her.

Alex set the controls down and picked up a pen. He flipped it in the air, deftly catching it as it came down. The motion made him concentrate on something other than her pale face, the brilliant glitter in her blue eyes.

Hillary pulled up a chair and sat down. For a moment they sat in silence, watching the motion of the train. Finally, Alex spoke. "You didn't say goodbye yesterday. I kept waiting for you to come out and join us."

Hillary took the accusation like a hit to the face. She flinched and then straightened, meeting his gaze head-on. "You were busy with Rocky. I had things to do. I didn't think I should interrupt."

"Why not? You knew you were welcome."

"Yes, but after our conversation, I was too keyed up to stay. I wanted to talk to you, but I knew we couldn't with Rocky right there. So I decided to go home."

"We do need to talk about a few things," Alex admitted.

Hillary almost smiled. "There's that word again. It seems to cover a multitude of problems with us."

"Problems that can be worked out." Alex leaned forward, his expression matching the intensity in his voice. "I had time to think about what you said, and maybe you're right about me not being able to say the words, but you have to understand that I've never felt this way before. I don't know what the rules are. I don't know how to play."

"It's not a game, Alex. And before you say anything more, there's something I have to tell you." She took in a deep breath, started to speak, but nothing came out. Alex tapped his pen on top of the desk impatiently, trying to give her a chance to speak, but obviously wanting to jump in with his own ideas. But she couldn't allow that, not until she came clean and there were no more secrets between them.

"Hillary. Let me start."

"No." She jerked to her feet. "I did something, Alex, something you're not going to like."

"What? You made coffee again?"

"This isn't a joke."

"I was hoping it would be. Okay. Go on."

She looked at him, pleading with her eyes that he try to understand. "Before I left your house yesterday, the phone rang. It was a woman, and I was going to take a message, because you looked busy with Rocky, and I thought it was just another one of your endless parade of girls."

"Who was it?"

Her voice shook. "Your mother."

Alex stood up abruptly, knocking over part of the train track as it crossed the path by his desk. The model train fell to the floor with a loud clash, the broken track dangling from the edge of the desk.

Hillary jumped back, one hand to her chest.

"No. I don't want to hear this," Alex shouted. "I don't want to hear it."

"She said she was your mother," Hillary continued with determination. "I was stunned. At first I thought it was some kind of a prank, but there was something in her voice, so real, so convincing."

"Convincing." He uttered a sharp bitter laugh as he echoed her word. "Yes, she can be very convincing when she wants to be. Why didn't you call me to the phone?" His voice hardened as he saw the answer in her face. "Because you saw your chance to get the goods on me, and you took it, right? I should have known you couldn't be trusted."

"You don't understand," she cried. "I didn't think it through, but when I went to meet her, I realized that—"

"That you had the chance of a lifetime." Alex crossed around to her side of the desk and grabbed her by the arms. "Did she fill your head with her woeful story, how she left Nebraska to make it on the big screen and got knocked up by some Hollywood lowlife, and how she desperately tried to hang on to her son but by the time he was ten he was just too much of a damn nuisance?"

"No—"

"Did she tell you that she sent me away but promised to come back and never did? But that, of course, she had a good reason?"

"No, she—"

"And then I bet she gave you the tale about how hard her life was, that she had taken the wrong path with alcohol but was now reformed and reborn, wanting only to make peace with the son she cherished all those years."

"Stop it. Stop it," Hillary said tearfully as he shook her shoulders after each painful statement, his body filled with a rage she didn't begin to understand.

"Am I hurting you? God, you don't know what pain is." He let her go so abruptly she almost fell. "You're just like her, so full of yourself and your own ambitions, too caught up in your own life to care about someone else. I was fooled by your candor. I thought finally I'd met an honest woman. But you lied."

"I am honest, Alex. Let me explain."

"Explain what? That the public has a right to know about my horrible childhood, my alcoholic mother and my life on the street? Fine, go ahead, tell the story. I never cared about it for myself, or for that woman who likes to call herself my mother, but for the kids. Did she show you their pictures? Amanda and Katherine? Pure, innocent little girls who believe their mother is a saint," he said. "Of course, they won't for long, now that superstar reporter Hillary Blaine can spill the beans and sell her soul all the way to Washington, D.C."

"She didn't tell me about her kids," Hillary said wearily, knowing it was useless to try to stop his tirade. He wasn't going to listen to her. And maybe she didn't deserve his understanding. She had breached his trust, maybe not as fully as he thought, but she was certainly not blameless.

Leaning over, she picked up the train from the floor. Part of the side rails had fallen off, and her eyes blurred with tears at the broken train and her broken relationship.

"Just leave it alone," Alex ordered. "Put it down and don't touch anything else."

"Not even you?" Hillary asked, searching his face for some softening, but his eyes were glittering with anger, his face stiff and uncompromising. Dropping her gaze, she fumbled in her purse for the letter Alex's mother had given her and handed it to him. Then, she turned to leave. She waited a few seconds, hoping he would break the silence, but he didn't, and she walked out.

It was over.

Chapter Twelve

Hillary walked out of Alex's office in downtown San Francisco and kept going, letting herself be pushed around by the late-afternoon crowd. She walked and walked until her side was hurting and beads of sweat were pooling up on her face. By the time she had circled the city streets and gone back to her office building she was no more closer to an answer than she had been when she'd left.

Alex's words continued to ring in her mind as she tried to piece together the jagged edges he had tossed out at her. His mother hadn't died. She had deserted him. No wonder he had made up a story. And then apparently she had remarried and had more children, the people that Alex wanted to protect.

She stopped walking, uncaring that two people bumped into the back of her and muttered complaints. That was it. Micky had said all she needed to know was that Alex took care of his friends. He didn't want the girls to know the truth, so he had turned himself into someone else.

But what did it all mean? Who was Alex Donovan? What could she possibly write about him in her article? If you didn't know everything about him, none of it made sense. Or did it? The questions continued to plague her as she walked into the building and took the elevator upstairs to her floor.

She had hoped to get to her cubicle without having to stop and chat. She needed to be alone, to think about what she was going to do. Unfortunately, Roger was standing by the receptionist's desk when she walked in. He latched on to her with greedy enthusiasm.

"How's it going, Hillary? Any news on our man?"

She shook her head, unwilling to meet his direct gaze. She couldn't tell him anything, not yet, not until she had time to figure things out.

His face registered disappointment. "What's the problem? There has to be more to his story than benevolent millionaire."

"What's wrong with that? You said everyone liked a success story."

"True, I suppose if that's the best you can do..."

They had reached the edge of her cubicle, but at his words Hillary turned around to face him. "What are you saying?"

Roger chewed noisily on a piece of gum. "Crawley just found embezzlement at the Tyler Candy Company."

"I see."

"I'm sorry, but if you can't produce, then I may not have a decision to make. The Washington, D.C. post can only go to one of you." Roger scratched his head. "I really did not stack the deck, Hillary. I thought I was giving you something with meat. Alex Donovan has always been a puzzle to me. But if you say he's clean, then that's that. When can I expect the first draft?"

"End of the week."

"Good. Then we can talk about your next assignment."

"What do you have in mind?"

Roger frowned. "I don't think I'll tell you until I see the story. I don't want it to color your thinking."

"Another subtle threat?" she snapped. "This article is going to be a damn good one. And I may not be able to tie Alex to a mob, but I can..." Her voice drifted away as she realized she couldn't even say it, much less think about writing it.

"Can what?" he asked with renewed interest.

"You'll just have to wait and read about it."

"I hope you can surprise me, Hillary. I'd love to buy you a ticket to the White House." Roger gave her a punch on the arm and walked away.

Surprise him. Hillary sat down at her desk and spun the globe. She could surprise him. She could give the whole world a thrill, because she had a feeling Alex had given her only the basic threads of the story. She could add color and pizzazz, tear apart his press release, show how he had lied to the public, pretending to be something he wasn't. The doors to high society would slam shut in his face. Some people wouldn't care. He was still rich, but others would sneer at his lower-class roots.

Roger would love the scandal, the unveiling of the real Alex Donovan, and she would get Washington, D.C., her long-term goal. She would be at the peak of her career, a respected journalist, just like her father. He would have been proud of her. Or would he? Would he have sold his soul for a story? Given up on love for the pursuit of a career?

She wondered what her parents' marriage had really been like. She had never thought of it from any perspective but that of a young child. Her mother had always claimed that they were madly in love, and her father had always returned from his trips with carnations and chocolates, her mother's two favorite things. Somehow they had managed to juggle the demands of his career and still maintain a happy marriage. But had all the sacrifices been on her mother's side? She used to think so, looking down on her mother's lack of ambition with the smugness of youth, but now the choices did not seem so clear-cut.

The globe twirled around, and she was staring at South America. Brazil. An old faded memory came to life. Her father had wanted to take the family to Brazil for a year, to accept a long-term post there. She remembered the long quiet discussions, the light burning in her parents' room well into the night, and then her father had decided not to go. Perhaps he had compromised along the way, as well.

But the question wasn't really about her parents. It was about her. Could she compromise, become part of a two-person relationship, give up her independence to be someone's wife? To be Alex's wife?

Somehow when she personalized it, the decision seemed easier to make. It wouldn't be hard to live with Alex, to love him every day. She already did. The emotion had crept in on her and caught her unawares. He had bridged her defenses, her fear of rejection. He had filled her with confidence in herself as a woman and created an intense need in her soul to make love.

She smiled at the thought that just wouldn't leave her mind. Every time he kissed her, he awakened a whole new set of desires. She wanted him with an intensity that would have shocked her just a month earlier. And she had a feeling that need was not going to go away. But somehow she would have to get used to living with the pain, because

Alex hated her. She had seen it on his face and heard it in his voice.

Reaching over, she flipped on her computer and waited as the machine warmed up and the blue screen lighted up her cubicle. There was no point in dawdling. She had to write an in-depth article on Alex Donovan, and she would. Her personal relationship with him was finished.

She typed in the heading, ''Alex Donovan,'' and then paused, her fingers hovering over the keyboard. She hit the return button and printed out the title of her article, ''The Man Behind The Magic.''

The next day Alex walked down the street in front of Fisherman's Wharf completely oblivious to the tourists eating lobster and shrimp out of paper cups. He was not on a holiday or even taking a break. He was on a mission.

He was going to meet his mother. He was going to look into the eyes of the woman who had left him twenty-five years ago with a stuffed teddy bear and a change of clothes.

His step faltered as he saw the sign for Pier 39. He knew she would be there. He had told Rosemary to call her and leave a message. A part of him hoped she wouldn't show, because then he would have another excuse to hate her. He didn't want to weaken, but he had to admit that the constant stream of letters coming into his house over the past two years had taken their toll.

In the beginning he had tried not to read them, but he couldn't get himself to throw them away, and eventually he had opened them up. Her excuses had only hardened the core of steel around his heart, but then the excuses had turned to explanations, and he had begun to see his mother as a person in her own right, a human being who had known pain as he had known pain. The fact that she had caused his pain was something he tried to hold on to, but the passing of years was dimming even that defense.

Since he had gotten to know Hillary, since he had felt exhilarated by another person's soul, since he had wanted to make love for hours on end, he had begun to realize that perhaps love made people do crazy, irresponsible, impetuous things. And he was a grown man. His mother had been eighteen when she had left home, a young impressionable girl with her head in the clouds. Nothing could have prepared her for the inevitable painful drop to the ground.

He walked onto the pier and paused. She was standing by the fountain, staring down at the water, a tall, slender woman in a peach-colored dress. He knew it from the way she moved back and forth from one foot to the other. She had done that the day she'd left, nervously expecting tears and protests. He wondered what she thought she was going to get today.

A pain shot through him, starting in his heart and spreading down to his toes. He couldn't do this. He turned away and then stopped, breathing heavily. No more running away. No more pretenses. Hillary was going to open everything up. The only way he could protect his half sisters was to alert their mother so she could prepare them for the horrible truth.

When he turned back around, she was facing him, an expression of wariness mixing with a painful joy. She reached out a hand and let it drop, and they stood there staring at each other for almost a minute. Finally he moved, walking over to her so they wouldn't have to yell.

"Is it really you?" she asked.

He nodded, still not quite able to speak. Suddenly he wasn't thirty-five anymore, but a young boy, wanting to know why she was leaving. He cleared his throat. "I only came because we have a problem."

She looked at him so thoroughly he thought she was memorizing his face. Nervously he ran a hand through his hair, watching her gaze follow his gesture.

"Only a few touches of gray," she murmured. "I've seen your pictures in the papers, of course, but you never seemed quite real. You look a lot like your grandfather."

Alex steeled himself at the mention of a man who died before he'd ever had a chance to meet him. "I wouldn't know."

"I have so much to say, but I don't know where to start."

"Then let me. The woman you spoke to yesterday is a reporter. So whatever you told her is going to be the lead story in *World Today* magazine in January. I thought you should know. That you might want to protect your daughters from the truth."

"She did say she was a reporter."

"When was that? After she grilled you about our life in L.A.?" he asked, bitterness spilling out of his voice.

"No. I didn't tell her anything. In fact, I tried, but she said she didn't want me to talk. At first I thought she was a girlfriend, or maybe even a wife, and that she could help me make you understand, but then when she said she was a reporter, I was confused. She didn't want to interview me. In fact, she couldn't get away fast enough."

Alex looked at his mother in confusion. It didn't make sense. Hillary would do anything to make her story juicy and titillating. She certainly wouldn't just walk away from a woman who claimed to be his mother. "You don't have to protect her," he said finally. "I told her most everything anyway."

"I'm not protecting her." She studied him for a long moment. "This woman is more than just a reporter to you, isn't she?"

"Not anymore." He dug his hands into his pockets. "At any rate, I thought you should know what was coming down, so you can talk to your children."

"That's what I'm trying to do today."

"I'm not your child. I haven't been in a very long time. In fact, I remember when you couldn't get rid of me fast enough."

She shook her head, her eyes clouding with pain. "Haven't you read my letters? Don't you know what I went through? I was young and foolish and drunk most of the time. I really meant to go back for you, but I could barely get dressed in the morning."

"So you want me to feel sorry for you?"

"No, I don't deserve that. I know that what I did was horrible. But by the time I got myself together, you were living with Stella. I used to watch you go to school with her, and you seemed happy. I didn't think I had a right to break that up."

"Then you left town, got remarried and conveniently forgot about me again."

"No, I never forgot. Never. But I lost track of you after she died. I tried to find you. I wanted you to come and live with me and Scott."

"Oh, right." Alex laughed in disbelief. "Then you would have had to tell him your sordid little story."

"He knew, Alex. He knew from the very beginning, and I told the girls last month. They all want you to be a part of the family. Maybe that's asking too much. I know you hate me. But I keep hoping that someday we'll be able to make peace, to start from now and not from back then."

Alex turned away, breathing hard. He couldn't believe what she was saying. He didn't want to hear about her love. He didn't want to hear about her life or her precious family. They meant nothing to him, nothing.

He walked away, hearing her call his name, but he couldn't stop. He was afraid of what he might say. He was afraid that by letting go of the past, he wouldn't know who he was anymore.

It was eleven o'clock at night and the gym was completely empty. Alex put on his boxing gloves and walked over to the bag. The first punch was for his mother. The second was for her lies. The third was for his unknown father and the fourth for all the foster parents who had made him feel like an outsider, unwanted, unloved.

He had been rejected from the day he was conceived, first by one person and then by another. Nothing he did was ever good enough to make them want to keep him.

Another punch and another, and his blood was pounding through his veins as he attacked the bag with the pent-up frustation of his entire life. Maybe he wasn't to blame. The idea had been occurring to him more and more over the past few years. He had been an innocent child, a pawn in their games.

He was an adult now, and he had a good life. Maybe that's why his mother had chosen to seek him out. How could he have hard feelings when he was a brilliant success, when he had more money than she could even dream about?

That was part of what had driven him through the years, wanting to prove that he was somebody, that he could be the best, the most popular, the most desired.

He hit the bag again, letting it rebound against his body in a hard blow, but he didn't even feel it. The word "desire" had triggered all the emotions about Hillary. He wanted her more than he wanted anyone in his life. But she had lied to him, betrayed him, used him for her own selfish gains.

His eyes blurred and he blinked hard, pounding at the bag until he could feel the muscles in his arms tightening in protest. Finally he collapsed to the floor in exhaustion.

"Are you done?" Micky asked unsympathetically, sitting down on the floor next to Alex.

Alex looked over. "How long have you been here?"

"Long enough to see you trying to kill yourself."

"If I wanted to die, I wouldn't have chosen a punching bag."

"No, I suppose not. Hillary called me today. Said you might need a friend. She found out, didn't she?"

"Yeah, she found out." Alex slowly got to his feet. "She even got to meet my sweet mother."

Micky raised his eyebrows in amazement. "No kidding. How did you arrange that?"

"I didn't. It's a long, boring story, which I'm sure you'll be able to read about in Hillary's magazine."

"Does she know about the girls?"

"She knows everything. But it won't matter. She has tunnel vision where her career is concerned. There is no way she will let anything get in the way of what she wants."

"Sounds a little like you."

"I don't trample over people to get ahead."

"Not anymore, but there was a time when your bitterness made you pretty tough. It wasn't until the first million came that you started to ease up. Don't you remember, Alex? Or do you just remember the things you want to remember?"

Alex looked at him for a long moment. "I guess there were a few people who got in my way, but I didn't—I didn't have anything going on with them, personally."

"You mean, you weren't in love with them."

Alex shook his head. "I'm not in love now. It's not an emotion I believe in." He rolled his neck from one side to the other, trying to ease the tension that the word "love" created in his mind. "Maybe I had a few thoughts in that direction with Hillary, but at least I got out before it was too late."

Micky stood up. "Lucky you. Make sure you lock up on your way out." He paused. "And just for the record, Alex, Hillary may be down, but I don't think she's out."

Two weeks, fourteen long days that drifted into the month of October. A lifetime had passed for her, Hillary thought, brushing the loose hair out of her face as the wind picked up from the nearby marina greens. She tossed her head, delighting in the freedom of the movement. No more constricting ties for her. She was not going to hide her femininity behind a tough, facade. She was going to be who she was, and nobody else.

She paused at a stoplight, taking a glance at the store window. It wasn't even Halloween, but there were already reminders to shop early for Christmas. Then it would be January, and Alex Donovan would be Man of the Year, but not her man.

Hillary crossed the street and paused on the other side, her eye caught by the wedding gown in a bridal boutique. She had never liked frilly dresses, but there was something about white lace that was becoming very appealing to her, maybe because she knew she would never wear it. There was only one man who had ever touched the deep, private part of her soul, and he hated her. She couldn't imagine loving anyone else again.

Which reminded her of what she had to do. Patting her briefcase, she started walking again. She had taken a bus halfway across town, but decided to walk the last few blocks to Alex's house. It gave her a little more time to think about what she was going to say after he read the article.

It was almost seven-thirty when she got to his house. She knew he was at home, because Rosemary had reluctantly admitted that if she needed to see him, tonight would be good.

Now or never, she decided as she walked up to the door. The bell rang, and she almost turned and ran. But there were some things you had to stand and fight for. Alex was one.

When he opened the door, her heart stopped. His hair was delightfully messed, his tie loosened around the neck, his shirt sleeves rolled halfway up his arms. Whenever he was worried or puzzling over a difficult decision, he always looked endearingly rumpled. She swallowed hard and took a deep breath. "Hello, Alex."

"Hillary."

"You knew I was coming."

"Rosemary is a loyal secretary."

"But you didn't try to stop me?"

He stepped back and opened the door wider. "You have something to say, you might as well say it."

Hillary put her foot on the next step and hesitated. "Are you willing to listen?"

Alex tipped his head. "I'll hear you out. Come in."

Hillary walked past him into the house. They mutually bypassed the formal living room and dining room and walked into the family room.

"Would you like coffee?"

Hillary smiled at the memory. "Only if you're making it."

A smile tinged the edge of his lips and then disappeared. "It's already made. I'll get you a cup."

Hillary sat down on the edge of the couch, holding her briefcase in front of her like a shield, only letting go when she took the cup of coffee from Alex. She took a sip and then another, wondering what on earth she was going to say. For the first time in her life, words deserted her.

"Well," Alex said finally. "Why are you here?"

She set her coffee cup down and opened her briefcase. "I thought you might want to read the article before it comes out."

Alex stared at the manuscript as if it were a snake about to strike. "I don't think I care to read it at all."

"Please." She held it out and finally he took it.

Alex looked down at the first page and started to read, reluctantly caught up in her opening words. The man she described didn't seem real to him. He was a genius at business, a Santa Claus for nonprofit organizations and a caring man, protective of his friends and his family.

He kept waiting for the disclosure, the bold-faced print that would say it was all a lie, that he was a pretender. But the sentences were shortening. He was coming to the end.

The last few sentences jumped out at him, and he read them aloud. "'*He makes magic with his toys and he made magic for me. Alex Donovan, Man of the Year. I couldn't think of a better choice.*'"

Hillary waited, holding her breath until Alex looked up. The hardness was gone from his face, replaced by a questioning sparkle in his eyes.

"You didn't say anything."

She shook her head. "It wasn't important to the story."

"But the public has a right to know."

She smiled at him, confident now in her beliefs and her decisions. "I don't think your life is a matter of national security, and you're not running for public office." She got up from the couch and walked over to the chair where he was sitting. Squatting, she looked him straight in the eye. "I never meant to breach your trust. I made one slight mistake. My impatience again. My terrible curiosity. Sometimes it gets the better of me. But I can work on it."

"You didn't ask her anything, did you?"

Hillary looked at him in surprise. "How did you know?"

"She told me."

"You went to see her?"

"The next day. I told myself that it was only to set the record straight, to prepare her for the journalistic meltdown of our lives, but I don't think that was really why I went. I wanted to see her. She'd been writing to me for months. The bedroom upstairs was for her kids, in case they ever wanted to visit, but somehow I never found the courage to invite them."

"You don't have to tell me anything about her."

"I think I want to," Alex admitted. "Not today, maybe. It might take years for all the pieces to come out. Childhood was not a good time for me. It was difficult and painful, and I've probably blocked out a lot of it."

"I don't care about your childhood or what kind of kid you were growing up," Hillary said, infusing passion into her voice. "I know who you are now. And . . ." She took a deep breath. "And I love you."

Alex stared at her and then ran a finger over her lips. "I love you, too."

Her heart lightened. "Really? Even though I'm not the perfect choice for a wife?"

"I'm hardly the perfect choice for a husband."

"But I can't cook."

"And I can't do plumbing, so maybe this is a good idea." He leaned over and kissed her on the mouth, cutting off any further explanations. It was a kiss of passion and tenderness, no holds barred, no defenses to bridge. Hillary wrapped her arms around his neck, holding his mouth to hers until she had to come up for air.

"I guess this thing between us is pretty powerful," she said.

"This thing is love. *L-O-V-E*. See, I can even spell it." He kissed her again on the lips and then the corner of her mouth, the curve of her cheek and the sensitive skin behind her ear. "I was just afraid to give in to this overwhelming desire I have for you. It doesn't seem to go away."

"I know the feeling."

"I was afraid to trust you, Hillary. I wanted to tell you about my past, but the words just wouldn't come."

She shook her head. "You don't have to explain. I know now how deep the pain was. My own rejection was nothing to what you went through. I was a coward for far less of a reason than you. I just couldn't believe that anyone could love me for myself. I don't exactly fit any stereotypes."

"No, you're full of surprises, including this." He held up the manuscript. "This is going to hurt your career."

"Maybe, but I'm hoping it will help my love life."

"Be serious."

"I don't want to be serious. I've spent my whole life being serious, going after that Washington, D.C., post like an obsessed woman. I don't want to move away. I can write from here, and I can travel if a story requires it. Right now I want to explore a new side of my life, not a new city."

"Are you sure? I don't want you to give up anything for me. I want us to go into this thing as equals, as partners."

"There you go again, calling our relationship a *thing*. Maybe you should just stop talking and kiss me. I'm in the mood for a little magic, and I know just the man who can make it."

*   *   *   *   *

Is your father a Fabulous Father?

Then enter him in Silhouette Romance's

"FATHER OF THE YEAR" Contest
and you can both win some great prizes! Look for contest details in the FABULOUS FATHER titles available in June, July and August...

ONE MAN'S VOW by Diana Whitney
Available in June

ACCIDENTAL DAD by Anne Peters
Available in July

INSTANT FATHER by Lucy Gordon
Available in August

Only from

If you've been looking for something a little bit different and a little bit spooky, let Silhouette Books take you on a journey to the dark side of love with

Every month, Silhouette will bring you two romantic, spine-tingling Shadows novels, written by some of your favorite authors, such as *New York Times* bestselling author Heather Graham Pozzessere, Anne Stuart, Helen R. Myers and Rachel Lee—to name just a few.

In July, look for:
HEART OF THE BEAST by Carla Cassidy
DARK ENCHANTMENT by Jane Toombs

In August, look for:
A SILENCE OF DREAMS by Barbara Faith
THE SEVENTH NIGHT by Amanda Stevens

In September, look for:
FOOTSTEPS IN THE NIGHT by Lee Karr
WHAT WAITS BELOW by Jane Toombs

Come into the world of Shadows and prepare to tremble with fear—and passion....

SHAD3

**Relive the romance...
Harlequin and Silhouette
are proud to present**

by Request™

A program of collections of three complete novels by the most
requested authors with the most requested themes. Be sure to
look for one volume each month with three complete novels by
top name authors.

In June: **NINE MONTHS** Penny Jordan
                              Stella Cameron
                              Janice Kaiser

**Three women pregnant and alone. But a lot can
happen in nine months!**

In July: **DADDY'S   Kristin James
            HOME**   Naomi Horton
                           Mary Lynn Baxter

**Daddy's Home... and his presence is long
overdue!**

In August: **FORGOTTEN   Barbara Kaye
            PAST**   Pamela Browning
                          Nancy Martin

**Do you dare to create a future if you've forgotten
the past?**

Available at your favorite retail outlet.